Christmas Greetings

BY
PAT SIMMONS

ISBN-13: 978-1503311053
ISBN-10: 1503311058

Special thanks to:

Andy Meehan, President of Development Solutions Global Inc., Christian Inspirations & Papier de Maison, for his insight into the greeting card industry.

Other Christian titles include:

The Guilty series
Book I: *Guilty of Love*
Book II: *Not Guilty of Love*
Book III: *Still Guilty*

The Guilty Parties series
Book I: *The Acquittal*
Book II: *The Confession,*
Fall 2015

The Jamieson Legacy
Book I: *Guilty by Association*
Book II: *The Guilt Trip*
Book III: *Free from Guilt*

The Carmen Sisters
Book I: *No Easy Catch*
Book II: *In Defense of Love*

Love at the Crossroads
Book I: *Stopping Traffic*
Book II: *A Baby for*
Christmas
Book III: *The Keepsake*
Book IV: *What God Has*
for Me

Making Love Work
Anthology
Book I: *Love at Work*
Book II: *Words of Love*
Book III: *A Mother's Love*

Single titles
Crowning Glory
Talk to Me

Praises For Pat Simmons

I love Christian Romance novels and Pat Simmons knows how to unlock the imagination and take it on a quick path of hope, love and Jesus. You will always find some sort of message in her books just like I found in Stopping Traffic. I smiled! …—*Tamara Gatling, reader*

"The passion of the author is awesome"—*reader Hazel Davis on WHAT GOD HAS FOR ME*

"I love stories with a strong family presence. This is my first book by Mrs. Simmons BUT it will not be my last!!! I was captivated from the first page. I didn't want the story to end…"—*T. Baker "aficionado of books" on A BABY FOR CHRISTMAS*

"This is the type of Christmas story I love--a book that shows the goodness and power of God and the goodness of Christians who follow Him. The characters really spoke to my heart. Filled with characters who were real and honest, the story unfolded like a special present with layers to peel away…"—*Lena Nelson Dooley on A CHRISTIAN CHRISTMAS*

"Mrs. Simmons did it once again. I enjoyed David and Valerie's story. An excellent example of Jeremiah 29:11 - their love was God's excellent plan. This story inspired me and the Bible study lessons as well as the sermons touched me and I was rejoicing with the characters…"—*Kenya "BRAB Online Book Club" on A WOMAN AFTER DAVID'S HEART*

"This book had my emotions all over the place in a good way. I cried for both Desi and Michael during this read. I felt tons of emotions from their story. Some parts of this book made me mad, some parts made me rejoice; some parts had me praying to God to heal them both. I have never been on an emotional roller coaster ride with a book before and I was really deep into my feelings. I felt the pain of them both and my heart went out for their marriage, sanity, trust and faith. I really cried reading some of the Bible passages because it was so touching how the story and the Author used them to bring healing to this couple…"—*Amazon customer on THE KEEPSAKE.*

"TALK TO ME is a great book! I am an avid reader and Talk to Me is one of the best I've ever read. I found myself laughing out loud - sign of a good book, grinning from ear to ear, and then saying "no she did not!" Once I started reading, I couldn't but the book down. The storyline was intriguing and the characters were well developed. I finished it in two days! You definitely will not be disappointed. Pat Simmons is definitely gifted to write a good story!"—*reader Leslie Hudson.*

"Simmons shines in this Godly romance. This avid reader was overwhelmed by the compassion written and scriptures that spoke to my soul. There were points that I identified with each character which led me to further investigate other scriptures. She uses family history, murder, prison, and postpartum depression along with scriptures to show God's ultimate sacrifice and constant forgiveness of sins. The character development and storyline pace will have you mesmerized as two families face their demons. CROWNING GLORY is a masterpiece of Christian romance which is definitely is a MUST read."— *Deltareviewer" "Deltareviewer" Real Page Turners*

Chapter 1

"Okay ladies, remember, we're all going undercover," Saige Carter reminded her accomplices, gleeful at the thought of being scandalous. From her home computer, she stared at five friends in the video chat room with her, one of them—Maxi Winters, she had known since childhood and was her closest friend.

They had all pledged their allegiance to her cause—staking out their area's stores to spy on customers. "Remember, be subtle. Whatever you do, don't bring attention to yourself or our mission." They were to target three cities—more if she had more commitment, but still, Saige would take any volunteers she could get. At thirty years old, she was finally about to see her dream come true.

The covert operation would take place at three retailers within St. Louis; the other two in their respective cities of Indianapolis and Kansas City. Saige noted the time. "We better get to our locations. Let's get our party started!" She grinned and raised her arms in the air like a cheerleader.

"Let's not get arrested," Maxi countered.

This was the day she hoped she'd make her mark on

the art world, like Brenda Joysmith with her figurines, Annie Lee with her paintings, and Harriet Rosebud with her stylish hats on miniature mannequin heads. True, Hallmark's Mahogany greeting card line was one of the first choices for Blacks as far as African-American cards go, but she wanted her cards to have such a personal touch that people could pick them out in a line up, or from a bin with hundreds of others.

But this was about more than her. It had been the Lord Jesus who had nudged her in this direction. Bowing her head, she whispered a quick prayer. "Thank You, for this is a talent You've given me, but in the end, let my work be a blessing to someone in need. In Jesus' name. Amen."

Shutting down her computer, Saige stood and surveyed her attire in the bedroom mirror. She had to dress the part just right. She wanted to look like any other consumer walking in off the street, so as not to draw attention to her subtle methods of persuasion. The black turtleneck always complemented her high cheekbones and her brown sugar skin tone whenever she brushed her hair into a ball on top of her head. Saige smoothed her long denim skirt, and then slipped her stocking feet into leather boots that added a couple of inches to her five-foot-seven height.

With her car keys in hand, she put on her black jacket and wrapped a colorful scarf around her neck. "Ready." She took a deep breath and left her second floor, two-bedroom apartment, which was twenty minutes from her parents' spacious home in Hazelwood, Missouri—a suburb in St. Louis County.

Crossing Whispering Cove's parking lot, she climbed into her Elantra. Although she loved living on her own,

Saige hoped to be married one day and fill her home with children—three, to be exact. Maybe it was the wishful thinking as an only child, but the man-picking was in God's hands. Until then, she had a mission.

She recalled the schedule she had memorized as she headed to her first destination: Walgreens. Next was Target, then CVS. According to Sunshine Greetings, her company, those stores should have received their batches of new Christmas greeting cards that morning, which should have included hers.

In less than thirty minutes, Saige arrived at her first location. "Yes." She smirked as she circled the crowded parking lot of the Walgreens in North County. Hopefully the greeting card aisle would be swamped. Getting out of her car, she strolled through the automatic doors. She took a couple glances down various aisles before making a beeline for her destination.

Walgreens should have twelve of her cards in various categories, whether they were sympathy, anniversary or Christmas—Saige had done them all. However, the Lord had led her in an unusual direction for a couple of the cards.

If her cards sold well, she would have a freelance career commitment at Sunshine Greetings, a small company in comparison to Hallmark Cards and American Greetings, which dominated the market.

Despite the store teeming with customers, no one was milling around in the greeting card aisle. Her shoulders slumped and her steps slowed. Now what? She couldn't possibly go and drag people from the pharmacy or cosmetic section to the greeting card aisle.

Okay, regroup, Saige Adele Carter, she coaxed herself.

Quickly shaking off her disappointment, Saige recovered and began to browse through the cards for hers. Her eyes misted as she reached out and fingered the 3-D image on her card that served a dual purpose as a Christmas/birthday celebration. The artwork of a snow scene inside a snow globe seemed so real. Opening it, Saige stared at the words she had penned.

The world rejoiced when Jesus was born. God gave us a King on your birthday, so walk in royalty as the prince or princess you are. She turned the card over and stared at her name. Saige Carter. She patted her chest in awe and mumbled a soft, "Thank You, Jesus." However, what she really wanted to do was commandeer the store's PA system, like in a Kmart commercial, and direct everyone to her aisle as if there was a red tag sale on greeting cards.

Caught up in the moment, Saige didn't realize that a woman was nearby and reaching for a card in the birthday category. *Yes!* She counted to three, and then put her plan into action. Saige lifted another card out the bin and inched closer to the potential customer. "Excuse me, I need a second opinion. I think this is nice, what do you think?" She shared it with the lady.

The woman was slow to respond. Saige gnawed on her lips. *Hmm. That bad?* She needed the feedback, so she prompted her, "I mean, do you think the spiritual message hides the birthday greeting?"

"Huh-uh." The customer shook her head. "No, I get it. Who wouldn't want to be born into royalty?" She read the card again. "Where did you find it? Are there any more? I need a couple." She gently nudged Saige aside to reach over her shoulder. She grabbed two and went on her merry way without a goodbye, thank you for the tip, or any other word. Rudeness never felt so good. Barely containing her excitement, Saige turned around and grinned. She refrained from dancing in place as she mouthed, "Yes!"

With that boost of confidence, Saige waited for the next target. It wasn't long before another woman—older—wobbled down the aisle with a cane. A couple strolled along right behind her.

Saige discreetly spied the customers' choices, and then went to work. She was smooth with her spiels, which resulted in another sale. She was about to go after another customer when a tall man wearing a Fedora on the other aisle caught her eye. It was the quality of the hat and its gray color that caught her attention.

She couldn't help herself from following his movement. Saige loved hats, whether on babies, ladies, or men. She always felt they added character and class.

"Is there anything I can help you with, ma'am?" a store associate asked, coming up from behind Saige, startling her.

Whirling around, Saige displayed a smile. "Oh, no. I'm just looking at your great selection." How ironic. Usually when she wanted customer service, a sales clerk couldn't be found for a mile.

By this time, the dark-gray-hat-wearing man had wandered toward her. His trench coat, of the same gray shade, was open and exposed a black turtleneck, like hers. His slacks were black, too, which gave him a mysterious, fearless, handsome, and confident presence. But she couldn't let his looks distract her. She was there to sell him on her greeting cards.

The associate asked him the same question, to which the man responded in a deep, commanding, voice that could melt chocolate, "Thanks. I don't know what I'm looking for, but I'll know once I see it."

Uncertainty—perfect! So what if he had a crack in his confidence? Didn't all men when it came to buying a card?

Saige tried not to draw attention to herself as she watched him zigzag from display bins on one side of the aisle to those on the other. He would definitely be there for a while, so she gave him some breathing space and detoured to the candy section for peppermint sticks—her favorite holiday treats. When she returned, he was still roaming the aisle. She strolled within a few feet from him, but turned her back. If she could only know what was in his heart, then maybe she could help him.

She was definitely over-thinking things. Maybe this was her cue to move on to the next location. Besides, she had overspent her allotted time in one store anyway. Her mission was done here. Saige turned to leave.

Daniel Washington huffed and rubbed the back of his neck. He had no idea what had drawn him to the greeting cards. He definitely needed help. Daniel glanced over his shoulder. Where was a store worker when he needed one? "Excuse me, Miss… Miss…" He called after the retreating figure as he fought away the distraction of her beautiful backside.

When she turned to him, Daniel's jaw fell at the sight of her. She was *pretty*. He blinked as he tried to remember why he had gotten her attention. "Ah, excuse me. I know you don't work here, but I guess I need a woman's opinion. I'm looking for a card for my mother—" he paused "—and for my sister, too … and brother." *Why didn't I just say my whole family?* Well, technically he had, she just didn't know that.

Instead of giving him an annoyed look at his uneasiness, the sparkle in her beautiful brown eyes indicated that she was more than happy to help him. As she walked closer, the woman gave him the warmest smile, revealing slight dimples. "That sounds like an adventure. Let's see."

Her perfume made him want to ask for a sample just so he could have it on hand to capture her essence. While standing behind her, he noted the small mole behind her left ear that he wouldn't have seen if her hair was down instead of swept up in a thick ball on the top of her head. *Nice.* Instead of big hoop earrings, she had the tiniest of studs in her earlobes.

While he was checking her out, she was asking him a series of questions as if she were a professional spokeswoman. He snapped out of his ogling. "Are they for a birthday, holiday…?"

"Reconciliation," he softly admitted, embarrassed that he had revealed his flaw and woes to a stranger. "Holidays are strained for my family—for me."

Nodding, she didn't say anything, but her blank expression seemed to scold him for being in such a predicament. Or maybe he was projecting his own insecurities. The 'holiday spirit' that surrounded him at work, in stores, and even in his neighborhood made him feel like an outcast at this time of year.

Daniel followed her as she crossed the aisle. He peeped over her shoulder as she began to select cards from a bin as if she knew what they were without looking at them.

"Okay. What about this one for your mother?" She

handed him a card that was colorful and had a picture of a treasure chest on the cover.

It was pretty and dainty, just like his mother. He didn't know what was inside, but he was sure she would like it. When Daniel looked closer, he saw the faint scene of a young woman in a bed, her children cuddled next to her as she opened the box. Immediately, he remembered the closeness his family shared when he was younger and his father was still alive. Childhood was truly like a fairytale. Once children grew up, reality set in.

He opened the card: *Mom, I miss our special moments… I'm sorry for staying away too long. Your loving son.* Daniel choked. All the words he couldn't say were written right there. He swallowed and nodded. "Perfect. I'll take it."

"Great." She seemed pleased, as if she had just earned commission on a luxury car he had just purchased. "For your sister…" She tilted her head and gnawed on her full lips, removing a hint of lipstick. Nice lips. "If she's anything like me, she'll understand that people who apologize are a special breed. Hint—*special.*"

Daniel needed to be special in his family's eyes right now. If this woman only knew about him, then maybe she would have some compassion. However, *he* wasn't the problem. *He* wasn't the one who had done something wrong, yet his family had made him out to be the bad guy – all because he refused to *give*—not loan—his married sister money to pay her house note when she had a husband who hadn't been able to pay rent for three months. Since he refused to be any woman's sugar daddy, he sure wasn't going to be a brother-in-law sugar daddy.

Without looking at it, Daniel was about to pass on a

card for his sister, but then the woman began to read in a soft, melodious voice. He was mesmerized.

"God gave me you. He must have known, despite our disagreements, our love would always be there, even when we're too stubborn to be the first one to say I'm sorry. We should talk." Glancing up, she searched his eyes, as if looking for confirmation that the card had hit home.

Bingo. It had. Like a reluctant child, Daniel gritted his teeth. "Okay, I'll take this one too."

"Excellent!" She said it with so much restrained excitement, Daniel wanted to laugh. "Now, for your brother... I don't have any, but I know men are such hot heads."

Folding his arms to look intimidating, Daniel smirked. "Is that so?"

"Yep." She was teasing him. "And most times, pride gets in the way, so I chose three for *you* to decide." She handed them to him, and then gave him a mock salute.

She was funny and her warm personality was relaxing. Taking her selections, Daniel stared at the images. One card had two boys playing with marbles. Daniel and his brother, Thomas, had once been inseparable and had each other's back, but things had changed as they grew into manhood.

His brother always blamed others for his not being able to keep a job, even one at a fast food joint. Showing up late, or not at all, was typical of his brother. Daniel had learned of his brother's immature ways while in his last year in college. Since Michigan Technical University was more than eight hours away, it wasn't like he had been around to enforce the rules their father had instituted when he was alive.

Daniel went home as often as he could, and when he did, Thomas resented the authority Daniel tried to administer as a father figure. The divide only widened over the years. The front of one card was simply an image of a handshake—an agreement, a coming to terms of sorts. The hands seemed to expand out of the card, making it real. He opened it. *Although we can agree to disagree, let's agree to agree on what we have – each other. Two is better than one.* Ecclesiastes 4:9-12.

A Scripture. Daniel had been too stubborn to pray about the situation with his brother. This feisty woman was right, but was this enough to close their divide? Neither he nor his brother really attended church regularly anymore, so Daniel doubted the Word would really have an effect on their situation. Daniel huffed. There had been so much left unsaid between them.

"What's the matter? I don't have another—I mean I… ah…"

Daniel shook his head. "I guess I have to start somewhere, right?" he said, more to himself, but she agreed. "Well, I better get this one too. You definitely know more about cards than me."

Then it dawned on him, his manners. "How rude of me to take up your time without being on the payroll and not introduce myself." He extended his hand and engulfed her long, slender fingers in his. They were a bit chilled. "Daniel Washington."

"Saige Carter."

"Saige Carter," he repeated. "A pretty name and a beautiful face that I'll never forget. Thank you, Saige." Shifting the shaving cream that he had stopped to pick up in the last aisle, he clutched the greeting cards that had not been on his shopping list.

With Saige supposedly solving his problem, he had no

reason to detain her further—bummer. Tipping his head, Daniel headed to the checkout line, wondering if a simple card with words he couldn't say was enough to open a door that had been closed and sealed with duct tape for years.

Once Daniel was behind the wheel of his Benz, he didn't start his ignition. He just sat there, worrying the hairs on his goatee. He slipped the greeting cards out of the bag and reread them again. Fumbling with one card, he noted the name of the artist on the back: *Saige Carter.*

What? He had been speaking with the artist, poet, or whatever they called themselves? "Saige Carter?" Daniel repeated. So, that was the reason for her passion with each card. Tossing them aside, Daniel hurried out of the car and rushed back inside. He knew exactly where to find her. When he veered left to the greeting card aisle, Saige was back in action with another patron.

Daniel observed her. She had a natural, easygoing manner with the customer, just as she had shown with him. When the woman walked away, supposedly with another Saige Carter creation, Saige glanced at her watch and spun around to leave. She froze when she saw Daniel.

He walked slowly to her and stopped close, but not in a threatening way, so others couldn't hear. "Why didn't you tell me you penned those beautiful thoughts?"

Tilting her head, Saige twisted her mouth. "Because it's easy to buy Girl Scout cookies from a girl scout, but would you purchase them otherwise? I didn't want you to get the cards because I was hand selling them." She lowered her voice and glanced around them. "Plus, if the manager knew I was inside pedaling my wares, they probably would have put me out and banned any further cards by me. You don't want to return them, do you?" Her warm, inviting smile was replaced with a panic-stricken expression.

"Oh, no." As fine as Saige Carter was, Daniel would buy anything out of her hand: trash bags, baby food, even Bengay.

She sighed and relaxed. "Great."

He liked Saige Carter. He found her intriguing. "How about taking a break and letting me treat you to dinner, a burger, or a chicken leg… a steakhouse or McDonald's? I'm available." Daniel couldn't believe he was hitting on a woman in a store; usually the women hit on him. His friend, Jason, would rib him for this.

"Sorry, I'm not—" she looked over her shoulder again and whispered "—I'm working. As a matter of fact, I should be leaving for the next location to monitor my cards' sales."

Daniel teased her, "You mean peddle them."

"Yeah, guilty." She blushed.

"Where's your next stakeout?"

She giggled. "Target, up the street. It was so nice meeting you, Daniel. I hope the words bring you and your family back together again." She was about to walk off, then laughed. "Oops. I guess I better buy something, huh?" She randomly slipped two cards out the bin.

"I'll buy more of your cards, so you don't have to," he offered.

"Oh, these aren't mine." She scrutinized the cover and back. "I collect cards. I always have, as far back as I can remember. It's a hobby of sorts."

This conversation was getting stranger by the minute. Daniel frowned. "Aren't you defeating the purpose by supporting the competition?"

"My cards are for others to enjoy." Waving, Saige walked away to the register, never looking back.

Chapter 2

I'm being stalked. Saige couldn't believe her eyes when she saw Daniel heading toward the greeting card aisle in Target. The man couldn't be missed. She guessed he had to be about six-foot one, two, or three. She was never good at guessing heights.

With rich, brown, African skin, Daniel resembled actor Lamman Rucker, with a dash of something extra. His walk was an attention grabber, turning heads, including hers, with every step.

Didn't he say he was going to get something to eat anyway? In contrast to Walgreens, the aisle at Target was starting to become congested with potential customers. More than she could handle. That was the good news; the bad news was nobody had purchased any of her cards. They were hidden, though, which could be the reason that none had been sold.

Dismissing Daniel, Saige did a little stalking of her own—potential customers.

"How many have you sold?" his deep voice whispered close to her ear, sending goose bumps down her arm.

It was at that moment Saige knew she regretted

singling him out in the first place. "None—yet." She gritted her teeth in sudden aggravation. "But I'm about to try."

"Need any help?" His childish expression reminded her of a little boy pleading to do a chore to earn extra allowance money.

So, the brother had charm, did he? Saige released the annoyance that was building and smiled. The two of them working in cahoots would only look suspicious. She could only imagine security suspecting them of being shoplifters or worse. "That's sweet, but no thank—"

"C'mon, you've made my day," he insisted as more customers wandered into the aisle.

"If you want to help, then tweet or post about the cards on Facebook." Why did she feel that Daniel was infringing in her territory? This was getting crazy.

"Already done. I sent it out on the way over here. Well, actually, while I was still in the parking lot. You know we're not supposed to drive and text." He snickered, and that was the first time she noticed his goatee was trimmed with precision around his full lips, as if serviced by a sculptor. "It was a worthy cause. I couldn't help myself."

"Mr. Washington, you'll only be a distraction." She pivoted to walk away, but stopped and glanced over her shoulder. "To other women," she added, scrutinizing him from the rim of his hat to his polished shoes—or boots.

"Right." Daniel released a hearty laugh, and then disappeared into the next aisle. Was she relieved or disappointed? Saige didn't have time to give it much thought as she cozied up to a mother holding a baby. As she was about to pitch her rehearsed speech, Saige could feel a presence behind her. *Lord, please don't let it be security.*

Finally, with curiosity that would kill any cat, she

turned to find Daniel behind her, engrossed in one of her cards, as if it contained a book of words instead of a few sentences. Then, all of a sudden, he began to ask women for their advice on whether they would buy it for themselves. Glancing her way, he winked.

Maybe Saige was the one being played. Daniel was a natural interacting with people. *Surely his relationship with his family wasn't as bad as he was making it out to be?* A few minutes later, Saige admitted defeat in her well-thought-out covert operation. While Daniel was distracted with some flirty females, Saige made her escape to her final pit stop.

Her friend, Maxi, would never believe how her evening played out. She hoped her other friends didn't have any distractions like Daniel Washington.

Saige didn't return home until after ten that night. She was exhausted and came to the realization that she could never be a sales rep. The rejection—she took it personally. However, the customers who did take her cards lifted her spirit. Then there was Daniel, who fascinated her, but confused her at the same time. Although she didn't see a ring, Saige wondered if he really had nothing better to do with his time than tag along beside her.

After making half a ham and Swiss cheese sandwich for a snack and pouring a glass of Eggnog, she said her grace, and then called her best friend after the first bite. She wanted to find out how it went on the other side of town.

"Hey, girl," Maxi answered. "Are you just now getting in? What did you do, police the card sections until every one of yours was sold?"

"You're never going to believe what happened to me."

"Whatever it is, I bet it didn't involve possible bond money. Girl, can you believe that the supervisor at CVS in

Bridgeton told me I had to leave, even after I offered to buy something? Can you believe customers were complaining that I was trying to strong arm them into buying your cards?" She sighed and *tsk*ed. "And here I thought I was a people person."

Saige couldn't help but smile, and then laugh. Her friend was an inside sales rep by day, at a major shipping company. Off the clock, Maxi had a natural easygoing personality, which was hard to resist. Well, except for tonight, apparently. Usually that was when her natural beauty kicked in. Saige guessed that hadn't worked either.

"You're losing your charm, Maxima Winters, but I can top that. I picked up a groupie, if there is such a thing with greeting cards. First, he offered to buy me dinner—like I would go somewhere with a random stranger." Saige rolled her eyes. She might be single, but she wasn't desperate—yet. Maybe she would be if she wasn't married by fifty-five. "Do you know he followed me to Target and offered to *help*? The women were hanging on his every word."

"Hmm. That cute, huh? I wished you would've called me. I would've had no problem trading places."

"Knowing you, you'd have flirted right back. No, I was working, despite trying to look as if I wasn't."

"Stalking *and* flirting? Tell me more," Maxi demanded.

"He appeared to be the complete package—complete—from his clothes, demeanor, and looks, but something wasn't right with him. He purchased the holiday reconciliation cards. Can you believe that?" Saige's heart ached for him. As an only child, she couldn't imagine being separated from her loved ones, especially during the holidays.

"I felt the Lord leading me to write those cards. I couldn't believe the company even bought them, considering they commissioned me to write humorous, festive, and upbeat material." *What was his story,* she wondered.

"That just goes to show you those words were meant for that brother."

"Maybe," Saige guessed. Finished with her snack, she dabbed her mouth, and then it was as if God was whispering in her ear.

Once My word goes forth out of my mouth, it shall not return unto Me void, but it shall accomplish that which I please, and it shall prosper in the thing whereto I sent it.

While Maxi was chatting away with one hypothesis after another about Daniel, Saige quietly meditated on the Scripture in Isaiah 55. Daniel was God's purpose, whatever that was.

"So what is this mysterious Saige Carter crusader's name?" Maxi pressed. A romantic at heart, her friend expected wedding bells anytime a man held more than a one-minute conversation with a woman, except her. Maxi may flirt, but she didn't settle.

"Daniel Washington." Saige thought his name fit him.

"So, did you give him your number? You haven't gone out on a date since New Year's Eve when I threatened you to go on a double date with me. I can't remember that guy's name." She snapped her fingers.

Unfortunately, Saige *did* remember Greg Bowers. He was too stuck on himself, so that was the first and last date she had with him. She wasn't as picky as Maxi, but she was selective. "Nope. No number."

"That sounds like you. Okay, did he give you his?"

"No. I didn't ask for it." Just like Greg from last New Year's Eve, she didn't expect to see Daniel Washington again. And she definitely wasn't going back to those store locations. "It was one of those odd occurrences, but I will be praying for his family."

Maxi yawned. "Me too. Well, girl, let me get off this phone. Working for free is exhausting." They laughed and disconnected.

Chapter 3

How could Daniel let Saige get away without a phone number? Hadn't that been his purpose for following her?

He had let his guard down with a woman—something he rarely did—and she had disappeared from right under his nose. That oversight had caused him to have a crummy weekend and he still couldn't shake his mood when he walked into the office on Monday.

"Mornin'."

Daniel didn't make eye contact with his colleague, the first friend he'd made when he relocated to St. Louis five years ago. Although they were close like brothers, Jason Adams still didn't fill the void left by Daniel's non-existent relationship with his flesh-and-blood brother.

"What happened to *good* morning?"

Grunting, Daniel placed his laptop on his desk before leaning on the half wall of Jason's cubicle. "It would be good if I had a way to contact Saige."

Jason stopped concentrating on whatever was on his computer and gave Daniel his full attention. "What do seasonings have to do with this?"

After correcting his friend's mix up over Saige's name, Daniel conjured up every nuance he could recall about her, from her passion, to her expressive eyes, to her melodious voice. It felt good to verbalize the emotions he had kept bottled up all weekend. When Daniel finished his recap, he quietly went back to his desk to get to work.

"Ah naw." Jason got up and followed Daniel back into his workspace. "I've heard of guys trying to pick up women in the meat department at the grocery store, but in the greeting card aisle?" He folded his arms. "Let me get this right. All this happened as a result of dropping by Walgreens for shaving cream?"

"Yeah. They had a sale." Daniel shrugged.

"Mmm-hmm, but you also purchased three greeting cards, which probably *weren't* on sale." Jason gave him a pointed look. "Then, like a sick puppy, you followed her to another store. Man, there are so many holes in this story, I don't know which one I want you to patch up first."

Ignoring his friend, Daniel tapped on his keyboard to pull up a file. It was a proposal he had drafted in hopes that his firm would win the contract to design five overpasses near downtown St. Louis.

Although Jason was one of those who believed things happened for a reason, he seemed to be amused by Daniel's turn of events. "At least Saige's got you thinking about home. I'm tired of giving you free meals at my mother's house on the holidays." Jason grinned.

There was no excuse good enough for the Adams as to why he couldn't be at their dinner table on Thanksgiving and Christmas.

As two of only a few African-American civil engineers at the company, it wasn't uncommon for folks to mistake them for relatives. Both were similar in height at six-three, and similar in weight because they worked out at the same gym, and they both had outgoing personalities. But when it came to family, their mindset parted ways. Jason embraced the good and the bad within his family, while Daniel lost patience with the foolishness in his family circle and stayed away for any festivities.

So for the past five years, Daniel had felt like an ornament on a tree at Jason's parents' house. He was just there for show. The conversation was always lively and the food delicious, but by the end of the night, Daniel would secretly yearn for Eloise Washington's home cooked meals. Then Daniel would come to his senses. To indulge in a Washington feast meant either drama or the holiday blues.

"So, are you going to send the cards?" Jason broke into Daniel's reverie.

"I don't think so. I was just caught up in the moment. I'm telling you, Saige Carter has skills. She could sell a cat lover dog food."

Jason's hearty laugh drew the attention of some colleagues. Once he composed himself, Daniel's friend chuckled and shook his head.

"I'm glad you find this amusing, but to send them would be like admitting guilt to something that isn't my fault." *No.* Daniel had to stand his ground, or else his family would lay the guilt trip on him like lathering extra icing on a cake.

"Stubborn. You give us brothers a bad rap. Maybe this Saige Carter was trying to bring out the kinder, gentler side of the big bad wolf." Jason clamped another laughing binge. "Okay, but seriously, my friend. You really need to get caught up in the holiday cheer and maybe this woman is an angel, delivering you a message or something."

An angel. His friend was definitely caught up in all this holiday hoopla. "Believe you me, she was all flesh and blood, from the perfume she was wearing to her melodious voice, to the way her clothes were custom fit for her body. She was definitely real."

"Have you tried to track her down on Facebook?"

Daniel looked at his friend like he was crazy. "Of course. That was the first place I checked. Can you believe there were fifteen people with that name? Some responded, but they weren't her." Daniel grunted. "Why do people put scenery, animals, or ASK on their status on their profile pages when they're on social media?"

Jason smirked. "And this coming from a man with…how many, ten or fifteen friends? You are officially a cyber-stalker."

"I'm up to fifty and besides, I find no entertainment in reading about people's woes, gossip, or videos on things that aren't funny."

"All jokes aside. For whatever reason, you purchased the greeting cards. Now put them in the mail. I've been telling you for years that you need to resolve the rift between you and your family. Life is too short. Maybe we all can have a Merry Christmas this year. Ho-ho-ho." A grin stretched across Jason's face as he strolled down the hall, whistling, "Here Comes Santa Claus."

It had been years since Daniel had gotten caught up in the holiday spirit. If he did, all he would want for Christmas is to find a five-foot-seven inch woman with beautiful brown eyes, a slight dimple and flawless skin. That would be his Christmas miracle.

Refusing to believe in miracles—Christmas or

otherwise, Daniel signed into his computer and checked his emails. The reason Daniel had been so successful in his career was he never let his personal business interfere with his livelihood, so it was time to change gears and focus on his current projects.

His workday was almost over when Daniel received notification that another Saige Carter had accepted his friend request and this one had sent a private message: Hi Daniel, it was nice meeting you this weekend. Be blessed. Saige.

Finally, Daniel was out of his misery. Checking the sidebar, he noticed she was still on Facebook through her mobile phone. He quickly responded. Would you like to go out to dinner with me this week?

Have you mailed your cards? she asked instead. When he told her no, a few seconds later, Saige answered no.

He doubted that she was purposefully playing games with him, but Saige was definitely messing with his head. He didn't want to have a Facebook conversation. Okay, will you think about dinner on Saturday or brunch on Sunday? I also don't have a problem being your greeting card assistant. Name the place and time, and I'm there. He was sounding desperate to his own ears, which he wasn't. But he really wanted to see her again.

I'll let you know, Saige responded, then as he blinked his eyes, she signed off Facebook.

Daniel hadn't expected to find her only for her to turn him down. Then it dawned on him that it might not have anything to do with the greeting cards at all. He typed in another message that would be waiting in her in box whenever she signed in again. I would really like to get to know you. If you're attached, then I apologize. If you are available, then I have no qualms about giving chase, if that is what you want.

When he returned to his empty condo in North County—not empty in furnishings, but in a mate—Jason and Saige's urgings of mailing the cards nagged at him. What had possessed him to purchase them in the first place? Saige and her passionate art of persuasion—that's what. He glanced across the living room at the cards he had laid on a sofa table three days ago.

Would he ever turn them over to the U.S. Postal service for delivery? Daniel had more than thirty days before Christmas to think about it. He continued on to his first floor master bedroom to change out of his suit and into some sweats. As he undressed, he heard the faint sounds of old time Christmas songs playing into the air like the tinkling melodies from a Popsicle truck. It was his neighbor a few doors down. Ben's condo was always decorated from roof to porch with lights, and he capped it off by serenading the cul-de-sac with tunes from the time he got home until bedtime.

At least Daniel wasn't the only one who didn't decorate or have a tree displayed in the window. Many of his neighbors were young professionals; only some had children, but most who didn't decorate were too busy or worked too many long hours to care. Daniel didn't fit into either category. Since his split with his family, holidays were anything but joyful, even if he did go through the motions with Jason and his family.

Fleeing the sound of Christmas cheer, Daniel made his way into his kitchen on the other side of the condo. He warmed up the leftovers he had purchased from Dierbergs' hot deli department. The rest of the week, he would dine out, or test his culinary skills he had picked up from his mom.

His mother, Eloise Washington, was a widow. His father had died on the job as an over-the-road truck driver Daniel's sophomore year in college. Daniel had been willing to walk away from his scholarship and take care of his responsibility to his family. However, his mother had demanded that he finish his coursework. Maintaining a 3.7 GPA, Daniel was determined to make his mother proud.

"Your daddy took care of us in life and death. We'll be okay. If I need extra, I'll work overtime to take care of your brother and sister," his mother reassured him.

Taking a seat at his counter table, Daniel blessed his plate of steaming mac-n-cheese, baked beans, meat loaf, and cornbread muffins. After the first bite, he returned to his musing. He would never forget the smiles on his siblings and mother's faces when he graduated from Michigan Technological University.

When he landed a high-paying position at Orbital Engineering, the first thing Daniel did was move his family to a better neighborhood, not far from the condo he had purchased in Palmer Woods.

Daniel thought that he had been a good son and brother, setting an example and paving the way for his siblings to follow...until his sister got pregnant her second year in college. Even so, Daniel did what any big brother would do; he talked to Phyllis' boyfriend, Lance, with a threat, then backed it up by his fists.

"You better tell me you slept with my sister, because you're madly in love with her," Daniel hadn't waited for an answer. "If I were you, I would think very carefully about walking away from the woman you care about. If you don't love her, we can settle this right now." Daniel had thrown the first and second punches. Phyllis got in the way before he could land another blow. Apparently, his methods had worked, because three months later, Lance had a ring from Jared's and slipped it on his sister's finger. As Daniel kept an eye on Lance, he apologized, seeing that the man really did love Phyllis.

However, his younger brother, Thomas, had fallen under the radar during his sister's antics with bad grades, bad crowd, and a bad mouth. Talking to him was useless; the threat of roughing him up was challenged. It didn't help that his mother had readymade excuses for her baby boy's shortcomings.

"Daddy didn't raise any fools," he mumbled, opting out of the past and returning to the present. "But that was then, this is now." Daniel didn't resort to violence to settle a score anymore. He had frat brothers that were now attorneys to handle his business legally.

Finishing his plate, Daniel cleaned up his mess. Going into the small home office off the kitchen, he signed onto his Facebook account to see if Saige had responded. She hadn't, but she was online.

Daniel wanted to see her again, but he wasn't about to give chase until she let him know one way or the other. He signed off and began to close his blinds. Daniel noted two more houses had put up Christmas lights. He turned on his porch light for solidarity.

With remote in hand, Daniel made himself comfortable for the Monday Night Football game. Soon, he found himself mentally drifting again. *Three years.* It had been three years since Daniel had made up his mind to quit being an enabler and took Orbital's job promotion in the St. Louis office.

He made the decision after the mother of all

arguments. "So how's this job coming?" Daniel had asked Thomas while savoring the taste of gravy poured over dressing. It was Sunday and everyone gathered at his mother's house for dinner—no excuses. It was an innocent question and a conversation piece once the attention was off Phyllis and Lance's one-year-old son.

Although his younger brother didn't show interest in a secondary degree, he had landed a job with UPS that had great benefits and opportunities for advancement in the long term.

Thomas grunted. "Man, I don't need that job. I was late and they put me on probation."

Daniel frowned. "That seems severe for one offense."

"But it wasn't the first or second time," Phyllis stated. "If Thomas would leave that girl alone, he wouldn't be late."

When Thomas disrespected their sister, Lance had jumped in to defend his wife's honor and Daniel had sided with them. Their mother took her baby boy's side. World War II and-1/2 broke out with accusations flying. The dinner was ruined and everyone retreated to their imaginary corners. Daniel became the bad boy for starting it.

It didn't help that before the night was over, both his siblings hit him up for a loan: Thomas wanted a couple of hundred and Phyllis said her husband was struggling to find a second job to take care of them. She asked for a loan of eight hundred dollars that Daniel knew she couldn't pay back.

His mother didn't have a personal request, but asked that he help his siblings. That night Daniel had visited the nearest ATM, withdrew the money for the borrowers and made up his mind, he was out of there.

It wasn't as if Daniel hadn't made contact after that, but it was always the same story from his mother—Thomas was trying, but just needed a little help. Pretty soon, Daniel didn't call as much and when he did, he never asked about his siblings. His mother would ask when he was coming home and Daniel always had the same answer, "I don't know."

The phone rang. Jason's call to complain about a referee's bad call, freed Daniel's mind from unpleasant thoughts. Saige had done more than make him buy greeting cards; she made him remember too much of what had happened in the past that a card couldn't fix.

Chapter 4

"I definitely must be doing something wrong. You pick up a hunk at Walgreens, and all I pick up is my prescription," Maxi pointed out over the phone while Saige was on her lunch break.

When she read Daniel's message earlier, Saige was convinced she stopped breathing, because she felt faint. Daniel's swagger, his polished clothes, and now his direct request proved the man had confidence, but she also saw a vulnerable side she doubted he shared often, or at all.

"So, why won't you go out with him?" Her best friend continued to badger her. Maxi didn't give her space to answer. "You told me this man was fine. He likes you and his private message from Facebook proves it. I say go for it!"

"Not so fast, girlfriend. Despite his most unusual shade of brown eyes, I saw sadness there. I kinda felt sorry for him." Saige paused and sipped her water before continuing, "That was until he turned into a stalker, of course."

"Come on. It's the holiday season. You said the greetings cards is your ministry inspired by God. You and this Daniel guy were at the right place at God's timing.

Single women everywhere want to see how this is going to turn out."

Saige laughed at her friend's silliness. "You know me, when it comes to men wanting to take me out, I'm always expecting—"

"Listen, you're over-thinking this. Call your cousins for backup. It's like you have them on a date disaster retainer anyway. If nothing else, go for the free meal and don't forget to order dessert."

Saige shook her head, amused. Maxi loved to eat, but her body never showed the calories she took in. "Maybe I will." She chuckled, thinking about her Carter cousins who had acted as bouncers whenever she or Maxi needed assistance from a guy's unwanted advances. Without sisters to protect, Reggie, Derrick, and Vance had no problem coming to the rescue.

"Yes, you should. Daniel sounds like he's anything but boring. Now, agree to dinner, and turn on your GPS for the Carters to track you."

Rolling her eyes, Saige smiled. "Bye."

Saige's message came unexpectedly. Dinner at six. Meet you at 54th Street on Hwy 67 in Florissant. Hope you can make it today.

I'll be there. Daniel grinned and typed back, almost bumping into Jason in his excitement.

"Hey, man. What's got you smiling after lunch in the café? Myrtle's tuna casserole is never that good."

Lowering his voice, Daniel mumbled to his friend. "I

have a dinner date with one Miss Saige Carter this evening."

They high-fived each other, then Jason cringed. "Then I guess we better hope there were no major damages to the infrastructure for the Poplar Street Bridge. A boat slammed into it an hour or so ago. Check your email and let's get to the site," he ordered.

Daniel rubbed the back of his neck in annoyance. When things didn't go as planned on a work site or unexpected things happened to a building or other structures, his team was called in to inspect the damage. "Since I was the lead engineer on that, let me pull up a copy of the designs and I'll head over there." He checked the time. Five hours until his dinner date. Daniel hoped no buildings would collapse before then.

The thorough bridge inspection took almost three hours. Once Daniel returned to the office, he was under a time crunch to double check designs and drawings on a new mall construction. The report was due before the five o'clock deadline.

At five-ten, Daniel was out the door in his Lincoln Cadillac and driving off the company parking lot. "Come on," he mumbled as he waited for the light to change on North Broadway, so he could get on I-70. Since when did St. Louis have Friday traffic on a Monday?

He kept eying the time on his dashboard. It would be close, but Daniel was willing to push the limits to see Saige again. He would be a believer in miracles if he made it to his destination with minutes to spare. The restaurant was crowded—again, for a Monday. Finding an available space, Daniel parked and checked his appearance in the rearview mirror before donning his Fedora. He climbed out the car and slipped his arms into his coat sleeves.

His heart pumped with excitement with every step. Clearing the double doors, Daniel scanned the waiting area and exhaled. He had beaten Saige.

"Welcome to 54th Street," the hostess greeted him. "How many?"

"It will be two, once my other party gets here." Removing his coat and hat, Daniel took the bench facing the door. Checking the time on the phone, he wondered if Saige would stand him up or if she was just a person never on time. He knew only one side of her.

Yes, she was pretty—no question, focused—too much, and apparently single. Maybe he could change that status if they could get a chance to know each other. Dinner was certainly a start.

The door opened and a gust of wind swept Saige inside the entrance, giving her the spotlight as if she were on runaway. Daniel stood. "Wow." At Walgreen's, Saige was pretty as an unassuming customer, though she wasn't, but in front of him was a stylish woman in full diva attire: the cap and coat alone made her a stunning replica of a model in a magazine spread. "You look stunning," he whispered, towering over her.

"Thank you." Her eyes seemed to sparkle and her long lashes fluttered.

Unbuttoning her coat, Saige exposed a sweater dress that complemented her curves. Evidently, she was a fan of boots. She wore a different pair that wrapped around her legs and stopped at her knees.

Daniel kept himself from groaning. It was going to be a long night, because all he would want to do is touch her—hands, hair, cheeks, hips, lips… Taking what he could get away with, he assisted her with her coat, brushing the nape of her neck. She shivered as the hostess approached them.

"We're ready now." He nodded and let Saige go first as they trailed the young girl to a booth.

"Is this all right?" the hostess asked.

"Perfect." Saige smiled and slid in the seat and he sat across from her.

Once they were informed of their server's name, the hostess disappeared.

Daniel couldn't keep his eyes off her. She had so many beautiful features – he didn't know which to ogle first. She looked at him expectantly, as if waiting for him to go first.

"Thank you for coming. You made my day."

"I was hungry." She displayed a teasing smile, as Ronald, their waiter, made an appearance and explained the day's specials and placed the menus on the table.

Both ordered salads and lemonade. Daniel went for the country fried steak meal while Saige decided on a pasta dish.

Once they were alone again, Daniel leaned back and studied Saige in a different light. Not as a woman who had come to his rescue while in a moment of despair, but as a woman who he was interested in pursuing and getting to know. "You have beautiful hair. You looked good with it on the top of your head and even now, one big braid to the side." He could sit there and compliment her all night, but it seemed like flattery wasn't getting him anywhere.

"Thank you," she responded as if she wasn't expecting the compliment.

"How was your day?" He was ready to learn anything and everything about her.

"Busy. I work at a university in the international student support department. Many of the undergrads won't be able to travel home for the holidays, especially

Thanksgiving, so around this time of year my job is to coordinate programs that incorporate the themes of the holidays from their native land. Every year, when I think I have the customs down pat, we wind up having international students from different countries, so it requires more research."

"Sounds interesting." He folded his hands on the table as if he were a student in the classroom, soaking in her every word.

"What do you do …when you aren't stalking people?" She grinned.

Daniel chuckled. "I'll have you know that I'm a first-time stalker, which was partially your fault. What man would let a beautiful, passionate woman out of his sight?" He winked.

Saige blushed.

"I've been with Orbital Engineering for eight years. They recruited me before I graduated college. I worked in Detroit for three years as a project manager before accepting a promotion in their St. Louis office as a senior project manager."

"Hmm. I'm sure it pays more than stalking." Saige lifted an eyebrow.

Daniel watched her playful expressions as he pulled on the hairs of his goatee. "Money isn't everything. Some things are more valuable."

"Like family," she said.

Actually, Daniel was thinking about her. "Maybe."

"Why haven't you mailed the cards?"

The cards? Not that again. He twisted his lips to come up with an appeasing answer, so they could move past those cards.

"Listen, scribble something personal and sign your name. I'll even give you the postage stamps, so you won't have an excuse."

Daniel grunted and shook his head. "I don't know what to say. You pretty much summed it up in the card."

She reached across the table and touched his hand. The connection was ever so brief, but the effect was enough to charge his heart to beat faster. "Hallmark has an online website that gives suggestions on what to add before signing a card, depending on the occasion."

"I never knew that. Then again, I haven't gone card shopping in years. There's so much discord among my family. I don't know if a simple card would heal deep wounds."

"Mail them and find out." Her voice was soft but it had the undertone of a challenge. "Holidays are meant to be enjoyed with your loved ones. For me, Thanksgiving and Christmas wouldn't be the same without my family. We have so many traditions…"

Daniel couldn't relate to her jubilance. "The last time my brother, sister and mother were together for Christmas, it was a disaster—trust me—and somehow, it was my fault, so I vowed I would never subject myself to that chaos again. Life is too short."

This was not the direction he wanted their first date to go. Usually, his job alone impressed women, but with Saige, it was clear there was more she would want from him. Daniel could feel it. She effortlessly made him talk about things he'd rather not, as if she was his therapist. Yes, the woman had skills, persuading him to buy her cards without him knowing it. She was good. He had to give her that.

"Never make a vow in anger, because you may regret

it." She paused as their server interrupted them with their meals. Saige wore a whimsical expression. "I wish I had siblings. I'm an only child."

"Thanks." He nodded at the server. "Sometimes, I wish I was."

"You definitely need some holiday cheer." Saige reached out for his hands.

He willing accepted them, expecting her to give a long, drawn-out prayer. Instead she blessed their food silently, or maybe she was waiting for him.

"Amen." She looked up at him, and then began to sample her chicken and shrimp fettuccine.

"Amen." Daniel grabbed the pepper. "I'm sorry if you expected me to say grace. That isn't something I do out loud."

After savoring a mouthful, Saige shook her head. "I didn't. At times when things aren't going right in our lives, we need others to pray for us."

Daniel chewed on what Saige had said while he sampled his steak's tenderness. "So what was your prayer for me?" He was curious.

"God's will."

What did that mean? He wasn't curious enough to ask as they ate in silence. Daniel wondered if he had blown both his first and second chance impressions with her. He rested his fork on his plate. "Listen, I prefer not to place myself in volatile situations where the outcome is not in my favor. Whether it's a job, family, or a woman. I know where I stand at my firm...and probably with my family, too, but as far you...only you can fill in the blank. What you see is what you get. I don't play games, so is there a chance we can get to know each other?"

Saige shrugged, then folded her arms. "You've been honest, so let me be frank. I don't know. Do you always pick up strange women in stores?"

He laughed and the tension that was building seeped from his pores. "Do you always pick up strangers in aisles?"

"Okay, you got me on that. But that was all about business—I guess you can say God's business. As far as going out with a man I know nothing about?" she paused and pulled her cell phone out her purse and evidently read a text. "Yep, they're outside now," she mumbled.

"Who?" Daniel frowned.

"My cousins—all three of them," she said smugly. "A single woman can never be too careful. Although I don't have any siblings, God made up for it with my first cousins—Reggie, Derrick, and Vance. They wanted to check out the man who picks up women in stores and then stalks them to another store."

"I told you, I couldn't let you get away." Daniel stared at Saige. He wanted to make sure she understood that his sudden attraction was genuine.

"They're really harmless."

Right. He would be the judge of that. "Escorting you inside, introducing themselves, and exchanging a handshake would have sufficed."

Their server appeared. "Is everything okay?"

Briefly, Daniel didn't know if the man was talking about their conversation or meal. "Yes."

"Great." He seemed please. "Do you have room for dessert?"

He glanced at Saige. When she shook her head, Daniel declined, too, and the server placed their ticket on the table and left. He wasn't ready for the night to end, despite the fact they both had to work in the morning. "When can I see you again?"

"I've got a busy schedule this week."

Daniel mentally did a rundown of his schedule. If the potential new client accepted Orbital's design tomorrow, then there would be meetings until the end of the week to hash out the details, which meant long hours, but still he had to see her again. "So do I, but I will make the time, even if it's a late night dessert."

"I'll call you." She began to gather her things.

Daniel wasn't convinced, so he countered, "I'd rather I call you, or I might not hear from you for weeks. Maybe we can do brunch this weekend." He gave her a pointed stare.

Scooting out the booth, Saige stood. Daniel got to his feet to assist her with her coat. She placed the fur ball back on her head and adjusted it to a sassy tilt. "You can escort me to my car and I'll think about it."

Daniel smirked as he read between the lines. "I have to pass an inspection, don't I?"

Saige winked and walked ahead and Daniel placed enough money, including a generous tip on the table. "Turn on your charm, Mr. Washington."

"I got this," Daniel mumbled as he opened the door to let Saige go first. Immediately, three headlights blinked on, almost blinding him, then three men about his height stepped out and approached him.

After Saige made the introductions, Daniel assured them of his intentions. They chatted for a few minutes until Saige shivered. "You don't mind if I get her out of this weather and inside her car?"

With matching smirks, the trio nodded, seeming relieved to get out of the weather themselves. Accustomed to the bone-biting chill of Michigan weather, thirty degrees was a heat wave to Daniel.

Before Saige opened the door, Daniel pulled out his smartphone. "I'm ready."

The wind stirred up some light snow on the ground and Saige shivered again. She rattled off her number and hurried inside her car.

Stepping back, Daniel watched her drive off, while the Three Stooges watched him from inside their vehicles.

Chapter 5

Daniel Washington was good-looking, evidently gainfully employed, and said he didn't play games. On the outside—a great catch. "But he's hurting, Lord." And with his sexy smile etched in her memory, Saige dozed off to sleep.

The next morning, her mind seemed to pick up where her thoughts left off, thinking about Daniel. It annoyed her that he was stalling on putting those cards in the mail. She added on another trait—stubborn. Didn't he know that Christmases weren't promised year after year?

Throwing back the cover, Saige slid to her knees. After giving thanks for another day, she prayed earnestly for Daniel. Then her morning routine wasn't complete until she spoke to her mother, who answered on the first ring. "Hi, Mom."

"Hi, sweetie. How was your dinner?" Adele Carter didn't waste any time. "Your cousins gave your dad a report last night and I got it this morning. Their first impressions were he passed, but you know Reggie, Derrick, and Vance are going to keep an eye on him."

"Of course," Saige chuckled. As god-fearing,

protective, and easy-going men, she valued their opinions. "They wouldn't be Carters if they didn't."

"Are you planning to see him again soon?" Adele asked in a tone that indicated she was snooping.

Saige sighed. "I don't know." She peeped out her kitchen window and noted the dusting of snow. "Do opposites really attract?"

"It depends on what the differences are. Certain things you should never compromise and God should be number one." Her mother continued to offer sound advice, which included an encore of what she had been hearing since her first date at eighteen and now twelve years later, Saige still indulged her mother.

"Okay, Momma, I won't forget, but I better go. The roads don't look bad, but I won't know until I get out there. "Love you."

"Love you too, sweetie. Remember, take Jesus with you. If you can't, don't go," Adele ended the call with her standard send-off benediction.

Surprisingly, Saige arrived at Fontbonne University without delay. She hadn't been at her desk ten minutes, when her office phone rang and Maxi's number flashed on the Caller ID.

"Hey, girlfriend. Before you ask, yes, I enjoyed myself last night and it appeared he passed the trio's initial inspection."

While chatting, Saige's smartphone alerted her of a text: *Thinking about you this chilly morning. I hope you're inside somewhere warm, while I'm at a job site, freezing. –D*

He made her smile, not because his message was humorous, but just because he had thought about her. "Hey, Daniel just texted me with a sweet thought." She messaged him back. *I am. Stay Warm. —S*

"Oooh. He likes you. So what's the game plan? When is the next date? I know you're busy this week, but for the sake of true love, I'm willing to forfeit our annual shop—"

Humph. "Are you kidding me? No man is worth me giving up our pre-Thanksgiving shopping spree." A couple of students walked passed her office and she waved.

"If you gave him your number, that means you plan to see him again, so when?"

"He suggested brunch. Saturday's out and I'm not going to stand up God because of another man."

"You're making up excuses, Saige. Sisters invite their future husbands to church all the time, and then pray like crazy they will get saved the same day."

"I have no problem praying for his peace and salvation—not because I want him as a husband."

"Hmm-mm. Then hand him over to me." Maxi chuckled. "Seriously, compromise. Invite him to church, and then accept his invitation to brunch."

"I'll think about it," Saige said as ended the call to answer another line. And it was all she could think about as she went about her day. Since Daniel had said he was working outdoors, she wondered if he was dressed warm enough as she sipped on a cup of creamy, steaming hot cocoa.

Soon, Saige decided to put herself out of her misery by texting Daniel with a counter offer. *If you don't mind going to church with me on Sunday, I would love to go to brunch with you afterwards.*

Her heart fluttered when Daniel replied practically right away. *Done. Give me the name, location, and time, and I'll be there. Oh, do I need to bring a Bible?*

How long it had been since he attended church, she wanted to ask, but didn't. Daniel was creating a soft spot in her heart. *If you have one, or you can download an app on your smartphone or we can share,* she texted him back.

I liked the share part.

Saige snickered. *I bet you did. See you then.*

Can I call you tonight?

She felt bad to tell him no, but she had an event at the university and then when she arrived home, she had to create cards. Her greeting cards were her business venture. She had lost track of time with Daniel last night at dinner. She could just imagine how his baritone voice would lull her to sleep tonight and she would get nothing done. *It will be too late.*

I look forward to seeing you on Sunday and talking with you before then.

Saige smiled. There was something about Daniel—he had just the right amount of charm without being overbearing. Well, except for when he followed her, but it was his 'no games' sincerity that she admired. She hoped she could influence him to catch the Christmas spirit and reach out to his family.

You have planted the seed. Now stand back as I water it, so it will grow in Daniel's heart, God reminded her of 1 Corinthians 3:7.

So God was telling her to back off. Since He was the One who gave her the words to write, Saige wasn't about to argue with him. "Then he's in Your hands, Lord."

By week's end, she had spoken briefly with Daniel at his job. She actually felt bad for calling him. Despite being in the middle of a meeting, he still had taken her call.

"Hi, I can't talk right now, but I'm so glad you

thought about me. I'll call you as soon as I can," Daniel said and disconnected. Saige didn't hear from him until late that night in a text. Sorry about earlier. Meeting new important client. Just getting home. I'm beat and barely have strength to get in the bed. I owe you a rain check.

What woman wouldn't give brownie points for those gestures?

Early Saturday morning, Saige and her mother, and Maxi and her mother, Grace, met at the St. Louis Galleria mall to begin their holiday shopping. The day was reserved for finding discounted Thanksgiving decorations and essentials. Adele, also an only child, and Grace had been friends since childhood, so it only seemed natural they had the same strong friendship as Saige and Maxi.

"Okay, ladies," Adele shared the game plan. "Let's meet in the food court in two hours, grab something quick to eat and then head to Target." Without another word, their mothers waved goodbye and scurried in the opposite direction, toward Macy's.

Saige looped her arm through Maxi's. She already knew her first stop. "There's a Hallmark store on this level, let's stop by there first."

The store clerk greeted them, but they declined her offer for assistance. They knew what they were doing as they made a beeline to the categories where Saige's cards should've been placed.

A few times, Saige glanced over her shoulder, almost expecting—hoping—Daniel to appear. Besides Maxi and her mother, Saige had never showed any of her cards until they were complete—artwork and inscription. She suddenly wanted Daniel to see her process.

"Who are you looking for?" Maxi frowned.

"Wouldn't it be something if Daniel walked in?" Saige chuckled as an African-American couple caught her eye.

"You have it bad. I would say the only way Mr. Washington would come in here is if he has a GPS on your location or you texted him." Maxi crossed her arms and squinted.

"No, I didn't. I can wait for tomorrow. This is our girl time, so keep looking to see if my cards are gone and then we'll hit the shoe stores."

Saige couldn't resist suggesting her card to another unsuspecting consumer. When the woman was out of sight, she and Maxi exchanged a high five.

"Would you come on? We're not on a stake out. Besides, I'm not leaving until I shoe shop," her friend demanded.

"All right," Saige complied, but only after buying a couple of greeting cards from another line to add to her collection.

The two lingered in several stores, more often than not, leaving with more bags of goodies. Not surprisingly, by the time all four of them had met in the atrium food court, they had all gone overboard.

They ordered from the shortest line, ate quickly, and left the mall for Target and Best Buy. "I still have to get home and take care of my husband," Adele mild-manneredly fussed.

Saige and Maxi exchanged amused glances. It would only be a matter of time before Maxi's mother gave the same complaint. "Mom, Daddy will be fine without us. He's probably hanging Christmas lights anyway."

Adele and Richard Carter had been married thirty-seven years. They enjoyed private outings as a couple, and all three of them as a family. Her parents were role models to judge whether a relationship was healthy or not.

Hours later, Saige had spent three hundred dollars easily on gifts, clothes, crafts for her cards, a few decor items for her apartment. Maxi wasn't surprised that she had even picked up something small for Daniel.

"Does this mean he'll be around for a while?" she mumbled under her breath, as they wheeled their purchases to the checkout counter.

"I wouldn't mind," Saige admitted.

"Ooh, do we have a winner?"

"Don't know." Saige shrugged as they waited their turn in line.

"Please promise me you'll give him a chance to find out," Maxi tried to coax a yes out of her.

Once the ladies hugged and kissed good-bye, Saige drove her mother home. Her father *had* been busy stringing together the lights that were meticulously hanging on the outside of the two-story house with stars dazzling from every window. Their yard displays only represented Christ—no Santa, snowmen or reindeers. In the corner of their porch was a scene of Christ's birth.

When she walked into her parents' house, Saige could smell the lingering effects of another task her father had attempted and failed. He had burnt something. "Hi, Daddy." Saige smacked a kiss on his forehead and then wrapped her arms around his neck.

"So, did my ladies buy out the store?" Richard teased as he got to his feet.

"Nah, we left some for next time," her mother joked. "And what did you try to cook while we were gone? I had leftovers in there." She pointed to the fridge.

As the two playfully spat, Saige helped herself to a sample size slice of sweet potato pie. With a week before Thanksgiving, her mother had already started to bake the desserts.

Her father sat patiently as they pulled out their purchases. "Do you know how your greeting card sales are going?"

"It's too early to tell. Target and Kmart are on a consignment basis, so for every one of my cards that sell, the computer scanner will alert them to order more." Before long until Daniel's name surfaced. "He's coming to church with me tomorrow."

"That's my girl." Richard winked. "Any young man who is interested in my daughter better have a whole lot of Jesus in him." He was serious.

"After service we're going to brunch." Saige added happily.

"That's my girl." Richard grinned. "Always make sure he has enough money in his pocket to feed you."

"Well, if this young man doesn't have any plans for Thanksgiving, we would love to have him," her mother offered.

"Thanks, Mom." Saige gnawed on her lip, wondering if Daniel had a problem celebrating Thanksgiving in general or just celebrating it with his family. Maybe he needed some Southern love in the Midwest. If that was the case, her mother was always ready to dish it out. Her father, on the other hand, would want to know what was wrong with a man who didn't want to spend time with his own family. "I'll ask him." For Daniel's sake, she hoped he said yes if he wanted to make a good impression.

Chapter 6

The wait is finally over; Daniel thought when he woke Sunday morning. He couldn't wait to see Saige again, so he got up and started his day.

His phone rang as he wiped the remnants of shaving cream off his face. Daniel recognized Saige's number. He definitely had to give Saige her own ringtone. "Good morning."

"Hi. I'm calling to double check if you're coming to my church today?"

Daniel hadn't given a second thought about not going. "Yes, are we still going to brunch afterward?"

"Yes."

"Then definitely yes." Strolling out the bathroom, he sat on the bed, then chuckled. "There was no way I was backing out. No games, remember?"

"Keep reminding me, and eventually I'll never forget that," she said in a soft tone. "Anyway, I can't wait to see you."

"Then I can't wait to be seen and to see you." Daniel disconnected and suddenly thought about his mother. He missed Eloise Washington…and his siblings. Even when he moved out of her house, she still had expected him for Sunday dinners that she had cooked before going to church. His mother would be glad that he was stepping foot into somebody's sanctuary.

Once family was gathered around the table and the food was blessed, she would always have her say. "You all should go back and visit church again. You might decide to stay." She would eye her children, but her stern advice had fallen on deaf ears.

When Daniel moved to St. Louis and his calls back home became too strained, so he slacked off. But despite his infrequent calls, Daniel never missed sending his mother money every month for whatever expenses she might incur. Closing his eyes, Daniel dismissed the haunting memories and stood to finish dressing for church. Whatever his reason for going, his mother would be proud.

Thirty minutes later, Daniel checked his appearance from his recently bleached, white teeth to his polished Stacy Adams shoes. He always wanted to look his best where Saige was concerned. Slipping on his wool cashmere coat and Fedora, Daniel stepped out into the chilly breeze, mindful of the snowfall overnight.

The church, Holiness in Jesus Temple, wasn't hard to find. As a matter of fact, he had seen the building off the highway. He had felt drawn to come, but never made the effort until now. From members in the parking lot to those greeting him at the door, Daniel felt welcome by their reception.

Daniel cleared the threshold to the Lord's House and was tickled to see Saige pacing the foyer. His arrival earned him a glowing smile.

He couldn't keep himself from indulging in a quick

assessment. She wore a dark gray hat that could have easily been a female version of the one he had just removed from his own head. The matching color coat dress was formfitting and teased her knees. Nice legs.

Closing the gap between them and mindful of the audience around them, Daniel lowered his voice for her ears only. "You look incredible." He felt like a heathen. First, he came to church empty-handed, without a Bible, and second, every time he saw Saige, she was a temptation.

When an equally beautiful woman called Saige's name and walked their way, Daniel thought he heard a scolding tone of voice.

You lack the power now to cast down those imaginations and bring into captivity every thought that is an offense to Me.

Since he was in God's House, Daniel didn't have to guess who was talking to him. Sucking in his breath, Daniel glanced around. Did anyone else hear it? Judging from uninterrupted conversations around him, apparently they had not.

Once the Holy Ghost comes upon you, you will receive power, God spoke again. Acts 1:8.

God isn't wasting any time on me, Daniel thought as Saige distracted him with an introduction.

"Maxi Winters, meet Daniel Washington," Saige said beaming. "This is my closest girlfriend."

The woman was a looker. Both she and Saige were of the same build and height. Where Saige had flawless brown-sugar skin and long curls that were stuffed under her hat, Maxi had a stylish hair cut that complemented her face and had fairer skin.

"You're the finest stalker I've ever met."

Saige elbowed her, then the ladies giggled.

Daniel snickered. "Thank you and Saige is the prettiest card hustler I've had the pleasure of stalking." They all laughed as he extended his hand.

"I'm her *only* girlfriend." Maxi waved his hand away. "I feel I should hug you."

Daniel shook his head, thinking about what had just transpired between him and God. "Ah…" he racked his brain for an excuse. "Saige hasn't even let me hug her yet. Sorry, but she has to be first."

Nodding, Maxi stepped back and winked at Saige. "He's a keeper." Facing him again, she accepted his handshake. "Treat her right and nobody gets hurt." The engaging smile from earlier was gone, and then she walked away.

"Should I be concerned about your bodyguard?" he joked as he trailed Saige into the sanctuary.

"Mmm-hmm. She knows self-defense," Saige said off-handedly as she led him to the seat where her coat and Bible were resting.

The uninhibited worship service engulfed the medium-sized auditorium, which was almost filled to capacity. There was that aura of peace he felt when he was around Saige, but the intensity was stronger.

Soon the praise segment gave way to the acknowledgment of visitors, reading of announcements, and the introduction of Pastor Earl Hogan. When a family of four arrived at their pew, they attempted to squeeze into a space meant for three. Daniel wasn't complaining, since it gave him an excuse to inch closer to Saige.

The massive choir sung a string of Christmas tunes when Daniel would have preferred to hear something gospel, more uplifting—anything that wouldn't remind him of the holidays. It was almost Thanksgiving anyway.

Christmastime was becoming more depressing to him.

"Good morning, church..." Pastor Hogan made a few comments before announcing his text. "Galatians 6:9 says, *'And let us not be weary in well doing: for in due season we shall reap, if we faint not.'* Now, depending on which end of the stick you're on, this Scripture could be encouraging or draining. If you have the means to help someone, let me encourage you to help them. God doesn't put a limit on our blessings, so don't do it to others."

A few Amens floated around him, but it seemed like God was still talking to him. Hadn't God seen how his kindness was abused by the ones he loved? Yet, the preacher wanted him—the wrong Daniel—to go back into the lion's den to suffer more mistreatment. Though having not read a Bible in years, Daniel still knew the love of money was the root of all evil, and it had certainly stirred the demons within his family. He wasn't feeling that one at all.

Pastor Hogan broke into his reverie. "You have success, but your family is in need of you. You have multiple cars while someone else is catching the bus..."

Saige's soft hand patted his as if she knew where his mind was taking him. He glanced at her, but didn't say anything. Saige smiled.

"Holidays aren't always happy for every person here today. I get that, because some people are never satisfied with what they have and desire more. What more do you want today? The Bible says to be content with what you have. It's in Philippians 4:11. Blessings aren't always in the form of monetary gifts. Sometimes, people need food, shelter, a job, prayers, and other resources...Then some of you believe you have everything you need, yet you don't have Jesus... "

The preacher forced a gamut of emotions to swell up inside of Daniel. He felt condemned for pulling away. Yet, he still refused to take the blame for his actions. His family had forced his hand, because he did get tired of doing good, and it seemed like nobody appreciated it.

"As I bring this message to a close," the pastor said a short time later, "what I want you to take away today is this: if you don't have Jesus, then you'll always be lacking— always. Come today for a lifestyle change. Repent of your sins…"

As others yielded to the invitation for prayer and redemption, Daniel stayed rooted in his seat. After all, he was only there as a guest of Saige and as a means to get her to have brunch with him afterwards. She hadn't set any other requirements on him. Once the benediction had been given, Daniel could only hope his exhale wasn't audible.

He faced Saige and stared into her brown eyes. "Thank you for inviting me. Your pastor gave me something to think about."

"I'm glad." She reached for her coat and he lifted it out of her arms and helped her into it.

"Are you hungry?" he asked, recalling the reason she gave for accepting his dinner date earlier in the week. When she blushed, he knew she must have remembered it too.

"Absolutely, so where are you taking me?" She looped her arm through his and they fell in step as they exited the sanctuary.

"I have a friend I work with that suggested Wildflowers in the Central West End."

Saige's eyes sparkled. "Good choice! I love their Skinny Napoleon and their sidewalk dining."

Daniel released a laugh. "In case you didn't notice

when you left home this morning, there are a couple of inches of snow on the ground. No outside dining for us today."

She pouted and then laughed too. He kept a steady hold on her arm as she strutted across the parking lot in her heels.

"We could take my car and I can bring you back here," he suggested, hopeful.

"I feel more comfortable driving," she said, stopping at her Elantra. "Daniel, I barely know you..."

"Then get to know me," he challenged.

"That's what we're doing. I would like that and so would my parents. Do you have any objections to being my guest on Thanksgiving?"

Actually, he did. He recently turned down Jason's annual invitation to dinner at his parents' house. Although they treated him as one of their own, Daniel couldn't help but feel like a charity case. But this wasn't Jason asking, it was Saige. "I would love to." Opening her car door, she winked and told him she would see him there.

Chapter 7

"Twas the night before Thanksgiving and it was sheer chaos in the kitchen at Saige's parents' house. Once Saige had told her mother that Daniel was coming, she went crazy fixing extra food. Despite the madness, Saige wouldn't want to be any other place. This would always be home, even when she was married with children.

As Saige shaped the dough into rolls, she smiled, reflecting on her brunch date with Daniel. She couldn't believe his answer when she asked him why he chose his profession.

"Legos?" She had repeated, thinking he was joking.

Daniel's eyes lit up. "My mother blamed it on my first Legos set. I would build something, and then tear it down. Growing up, I always knew one present under the tree would be more Legos—Santa's Workshop set, Star Wars adventures—the more complex, the better."

Saige was enthralled as he painted a picture before her eyes of a happy childhood while she enjoyed her Skinny Napoleon, a concoction with scrambled egg whites, sautéed organic baby spinach, and other side dishes.

"Eventually, I designed furniture for my bedroom that I shared," he choked, "with my brother. Next, I designed and built a two story clubhouse that my sister decorated…" his voice faded. "My father was still alive and he showed me how to make sure everything I built was durable."

The more Daniel reminisced about his childhood, the more she understood his loss. *God, please help him find his way home*, she silently prayed.

"My father died before I finished college. He didn't leave my mother wealthy, but she receives a monthly check to keep right above the poverty line. Since I've graduated from college, I've had sure she's never in need of anything."

The mood was about to crash, so Saige quickly took over. "As a girl, my mother and I shared craft projects. When I grew up, I continued to sew, piece, and recycle things. It wasn't until a few years ago while reading my Bible, I began to jot down scriptures to memorize as an aid to study God's Word. Then, one day, I found myself in a greeting card aisle in awe of other people's words of expression, reading one card after another like someone would read a magazine—"

"See, a kindred spirit." His smile was genuine, and she relaxed.

"I guess we are. Before long I wanted to write something with beautiful words."

In an unexpected move, Daniel brought one of her hands to his mouth and brushed a soft kiss on it. He didn't release her as he engulfed both her hands in his. They were strong, yet gentle, and Saige didn't have the power to protest the touch. He had been right, the more she got to know him, the more she wanted to be with him, which was why she agreed to a movie later that evening.

"Shall I pick you up?" he asked.

Holding hands was one thing, but one dinner and brunch wasn't enough to convince her to let her guard down. There were too many horror stories about date rape, abduction, assault, and more. Saige held her ground on that one. "I'm not there yet. It's like a first kiss. I'll let you know when."

The memory faded as Saige seemed to float back to the present. She giggled, recalling how his nostrils had flared and his eyes brightened with anticipation. She shouldn't have teased him like that. She chuckled louder.

"Hmm. I don't know what's on your mind, but I've never heard my daughter laugh, chuckle and giggle all in the span of five minutes." Her mother gave her a knowing look.

"Daniel," they said in unison.

"It's about time some young man snagged your attention. I'm glad he makes you happy. Your father and I can't wait to meet him."

"Me either." Saige was about to prepare another pan with rolls but realized every counter and table space was spoken for. "Why are we preparing all this food?"

"More families are in need this year, so everyone in our auxiliary is preparing ten extra baskets on top of the four we normally do."

Saige's heart dropped at the news. That was a lot of people doing without. "No wonder you started cooking last week. You should have called me to come and help."

"It's no big deal. I cook a lot anyway since we usually get drop-bys from neighbors, church folks, and friends. When your cousins found out that Daniel was coming, they invited themselves." Her mother smirked. "I got it done. Your father even helped." They exchanged amused looks.

His help meant taste-testing samples.

Daniel would be able to hold his own. She liked that air of confidence about him. Nothing seemed to intimidate him, except his family discord, but she hadn't stopped praying for him. "I'm glad he accepted my invitation, but I can't imagine being away from family for the holidays."

"I know." Her mother paused as if she was thinking. "I have such great memories of every holiday with my mom and dad. And we didn't have a lot of money to celebrate, like when I turned twenty-one—"

"And your parents didn't have money for a big party," Saige stated, having heard the story countless time, "so grandma gathered twenty-one of your friends, family, co-workers, and church members with the help of Maxi's mom to call and wish you Happy Birthday at synchronized times."

Money wasn't the issue when Saige turned sixteen *and* twenty, but her parents thought it would be a fun experience to do it for her and it was." She eyed her mother who had a mischievous gleam to her eyes. "I'm good for thirty, so don't even think about it."

"Just because you're grown doesn't mean you can't have fun." Adele sighed and a faraway look came into her eyes. "I hope you will continue to pass on those traditions when you have your family."

"I will," Saige assured her as her cell phone rang. She peeked at the caller.

"I see you smiling" her mother said. "Go ahead, take a break and talk to Daniel."

Excusing herself, Saige didn't argue. She quickly wiped her hands and answered before the last ring took him to voice mail. "Hey."

"How are you?" Daniel asked. "Were you busy?"

"Happy." And it was because of him. "I'm cooking and chatting with my mother about you."

"If only I could be a fly on that wall," Daniel paused. "I can't wait to meet your parents tomorrow. Should I bring a dish?"

"Can you cook?" When he answered no, Saige laughed.

"Hey, it's polite to ask," he defended.

"Just bring yourself and come early. By the way, my cousins will be here, so you'll have a chance to spend some quality time with them again," she teased.

"The focus of my quality time is you, so don't even think about pulling a disappearing act or hiding out in the kitchen or whatever you women do."

"Right." Curiosity got the best of Saige when she whispered, "Don't you miss your family a little?"

"I try not to think about it."

An urge so strong came over Saige that she wanted to kiss Daniel and make all his woes better. Unfortunately, the discord between him and his family was something that only God could mend, as the Lord watered the words He gave her to put in the cards. They chatted a few more minutes before Saige ended the call to resume helping her mother. "See you tomorrow."

The next day, the smell of turkey and dressing ushered in Thanksgiving while Saige prepared breakfast for her parents. It was a tradition she had started since she was old enough to learn the safety procedures when cooking.

Daniel was the first guest to arrive a few hours later. He carried a couple of bottles of sparkling juice. Once she hung his coat, Saige held her arms open for a hug and

Daniel didn't disappoint. His first kiss was delivered in the crown of her hair.

Her mother was impressed with Daniel minutes after the introduction, and she let Saige know that when they were alone in the kitchen. "He might be the one, sweetie."

Saige wanted to believe that. "He's a good catch and all, except for his family ties, and you know that is important to me—us." She twisted her lips in disappointment.

"We know that the fervent prayer of the righteous avails much. We just need to stay on our knees."

James 5:16. Saige knew that was the second part of the Scripture. It was the confessing part people had problems with, especially in the case where they thought they were right and the others were wrong. "I think he's holding out for the Lord to change *them*."

Her mother wiped her hands and hugged Saige. "Honey, God doesn't always change situations, but he can change us while we're in that situation." Adele used her finger to tilt Saige's chin up. "Now, smile. We work under God's timing, not the other way around."

"I know." Saige sighed and finished her task and helped set the table. Another tradition of the Carters was they never waited on others to arrive to eat. If guests weren't there by two in the afternoon, they would chow down without them.

Walking into the living room to announce dinner, Saige noticed her cousins had arrived and the atmosphere seemed relaxed. That was a good sign. It had taken her father a little longer to warm up to Daniel, but his acceptance was apparent. Daniel must have given the right answers to a series of questions.

When Daniel smiled at her, he ignited the attraction stirring in her. "Come on, dinner is served." Reaching for his hand, Saige tugged him to his feet.

"Just when I was learning all the secrets you don't want to tell me," he whispered.

Saige playfully elbowed him the side. "I can't believe those Carter men would divulge anything." Her oldest cousin, Derrick, usually listened. Daniel must have passed another inspection.

"I'm really glad I came. Your parents are close to perfection."

Saige's heart fluttered at the compliment. "I think so."

Once her father had blessed the food, they ate, talked, laughed, joked, rested, then returned for seconds. When Daniel helped himself to a second slice of pecan pie, Saige was beside him, and she felt a sensation—the realization that Daniel Washington *fit*. She was completely comfortable around him.

He must have felt it too, because he turned and winked at her.

Soon Maxi and her mother stopped by to wish holiday greetings. The men took that as a cue to head to the kitchen and start the cleanup.

Saige rolled her eyes as the lively discussion of football from the kitchen drowned out their conversation.

By the time the men finished their chores, Maxi and her mother had said their goodbyes, so they could visit other friends. Maxi hugged Saige. "Fall in love, will ya?" she teased as they left.

Who knows, I just might, Saige thought. Minutes later, Daniel reappeared and she nudged him toward a study cove in the back of the house. After turning on the gas logs in the faux fireplace, they got comfortable on the roomy cushioned window seat in the bay area. It gave them a fantastic view of the light snow that had begun to fall against the backdrop of the houses that were now decorated in festive colors.

Daniel reached out and twisted her hair around his finger. He seemed fascinated with it. "You are so beautiful." His eyes softened with his declaration of affection.

She was mesmerized. "I'm so glad you came," she whispered. "I already know about the unhappy things in your life. What about those things that make you happy—things you're thankful for whether it is the holidays or not?"

"Meeting you, hands down." Daniel didn't blink. She rubbed her hand against his jaw that was void of any razor mishaps. "You are by far the most refreshing, beautiful, and unassuming woman I've met in a long time. Unwittingly, I've shared more with you in the past few weeks than I have with any woman. You're like the hot chocolate on a cold wintry night that you never want to finish."

Saige couldn't contain her blush. "Stop trying to charm me."

"Why? You've already charmed me." Daniel lifted an eyebrow.

She didn't know how long they talked about their fears, failures, and faith when her mother brought them a cup of hot chocolate. Accepting the mugs, she and Daniel shared a knowing smile.

"Your cousins are gone, and your dad and I are turning in. Daniel, it was nice meeting you. I'm sure we'll see more of you."

Getting to his feet, he gave her mother a lopsided grin. "Most definitely, it was nice meeting you and Mr. Carter as well. Thanks for the hot chocolate. I was craving a cup earlier."

Saige giggled as Daniel saluted his mother. Somehow, the hot chocolate had become their hour glass, and neither were in a hurry to finish and call it a night.

Chapter 8

Daniel was having one doozy of a Saige hangover after spending time with her all day. She was definitely who he wanted, but was the feeling mutual? Daniel knew he couldn't win her heart until he made the first step to mend his broken family. He had to go home for Christmas. Pride could no longer keep him away.

Sitting in his kitchen, Daniel sipped on a cup of hot chocolate instead of coffee, because it reminded him of Saige. He stared at the greeting cards. Reaching for his pen, he signed his name. He had nothing more to add to what Saige had written so eloquently. Daniel whispered a prayer as he addressed the envelopes and sealed them. "Jesus, I heard if I take one step you'll take two. I need You to make a big leap on this."

I stand at the door and knock, Daniel. Remove yourself, open the door and I will step in.

He recognized that it was God's voice, but what did He mean? Daniel bowed his head to contemplate. How could he remove himself when he was trying to open a door that had been shut for years between him and his family?

He had never been a philosopher, so, unless God made it plain and simple, he didn't get it.

Dismissing the riddle, he texted Saige. It was almost ten in the morning. She had informed him last night that she and Maxi would be hitting the stores for Early Bird Black Friday specials that started at five a.m. The two friends were doing it just for the thrill of the hunt.

I'm putting the cards in the mail. Pray that something will change.

Consider it done. Those were God's Words on those cards. Open yourself up to God and He will bless you, she texted back.

Open the door? Daniel's heart raced at her choice of words. Instead of texting back, he called her. "Hey, having fun?" He rinsed his mug out and reached for his jacket that was dangling from a nearby wall hook in the kitchen.

"Actually, I am."

There was so much noise, Daniel had to strain his hearing. Clearly Maxi and Saige had plenty of company. "Listen, I'm sorry to interrupt…"

"Oh, no you're not. Hi, Daniel," Maxi said in the background.

"Girl, hush." She paused. "Sorry, I had you on speaker phone so I could hear. You can interrupt me any time you want to talk."

Daniel grinned. "That's good to know. I called because I think God has been speaking to me lately." He repeated what he thought he heard.

"The Lord talks to us all the time. It's we who don't take the time to listen. Revelation 3:20, basically God is extending His own personal altar call to you. Open the door. Okay?" Her voice was so soft and soothing. "I've got to go. Maxi is waving to get my attention and pointing to some sweaters."

"Enjoy yourself and don't forget to shop the greeting card aisle." Daniel chuckled.

She giggled. "You know that was my first stop. Bye."

After Daniel dropped the cards in the mail, he didn't want to return to his lonely condo. Against better judgment, he braved the crowds in one shopping plaza. Daniel circled the lot until a parking spot opened. Out of the car, he stepped with one goal in mind. For the first time in years, he actually looked forward to Christmas shopping instead of going through the motions out of obligation to his coworkers.

A book store was his first stop, and then any other place along the strip that might sell greeting cards. What he thought would be a quick trip, turned out to be hours as he read one card after another, looking for the words he felt for Saige. Some cards were funny; others were for moments that had never happened between them like their first kiss, dance, wedding, and baby. There were occasions he had never heard of before.

One image seemed to stay with Daniel when he stopped at Papyrus. The African-American woman who graced the cover was on a swing and a handsome guy, which of course, would be him, was pushing her. They both were laughing and the scene seemed carefree. Inside the card, it read: *You make me soar.* He bought it and several others and even purchased a new Bible.

That evening, Daniel read and reread Revelation 3. Was God calling him out in verses 16-18 when he addressed the church in Laodicea that read: *Because you are lukewarm—neither hot nor cold— I am about to spit you out of my mouth. You say, 'I am rich; I have acquired wealth and do not need a thing.' But you do not realize that you are wretched, pitiful, poor, blind, and naked?*

God's scolding sounded similar to Saige's pastor's message. So Daniel had to decide whether he was going to be a Christian or not. As a matter of need, honestly with his salary, Daniel thought he had everything at his fingertips. However, Jesus didn't seem impressed with his resume. Before going to bed, Daniel prayed for guidance.

The following Sunday, he slid into the pew next to Saige whom he told he was coming. "Good morning."

Her eyes watered. "I'm so happy to see you." She squeezed his hand and didn't let go, even when it seemed she wanted to stand. Today, red was her choice of color and the dress looked stunning against her skin.

"I brought my Bible this time," he whispered.

"I wouldn't have minded sharing."

"You've shared Christ and that is priceless."

Before Daniel could say more, the pastor stood at the podium as the choir finished their song. "Praise the Lord, church and I hope you enjoyed your Thanksgiving with thanks in your heart. This morning's text is from 1 John 3:7 and 8: *Little children, make sure no one deceives you; the one who practices righteousness is righteous, just as He is righteous; the one who practices sin is of the devil; for the devil has sinned from the beginning.*" He read the next passage very slowly, "*The Son of God appeared for this purpose, to destroy the works of the devil…*this one verse should be the reason you celebrate Christmas, because the devil is going down."

He paused to rejoice in dance. "So be the light at Christmas, and I'm not talking about what you have stringing from a tree. Let the world see there is a difference in you this holiday season. Be Christ-like to one another, even as others are fighting over a toy. Spend money to bless others. You may only have one shot at this. Make it your best one." Closing his Bible, Pastor Hogan asked the congregation to stand.

"So there you have it, the true purpose of Christmas. God took on flesh in a one size fits all to die for us. You don't need to be depressed about what you have or don't have this Christmas. The present Jesus has for you is not under a tree. If you want to be righteous today, repent in your heart and confess your sins with your lips unto God, then come to the front where the ministers are waiting to pray for you. Complete the salvation process and let God wash your dirty sins away in the water baptism in Jesus' name. Once your soul is clean, He is ready to give you some keeping power with the baptism of the Holy Ghost with evidence of a heavenly language of speaking in unknown tongues. Won't you come?"

He wanted to say yes, but something held him back. Saige squeezed his hand and bowed her head. Her lips moved in an apparent whispered prayer.

Suddenly, the surety of what God required of him hit Daniel. Loosening her hand, he made his way to the front where a minister greeted him and asked, "What can I pray for you today?"

"I want to be saved. I want to be set free of the despair that has been clinging to me. It's time," he said with conviction.

"Then you want Jesus," the man simply stated, instructing him to lift his hands to God. When the minister laid his hands on Daniel's forehead, he closed his eyes. The man really prayed until Daniel's burden seemed lighter.

Why did his face feel wet? He hadn't realized that there were tears on his face. Shamefully, he wiped at them.

"It's okay, brother. When God strips us of our pride, it humbles us. You're shedding tears, but the Lord shed His blood. Do you want the baptism in Jesus' name?"

Daniel's voice was weak when he consented to everything God had for him. Led to a small room separate from the sanctuary, someone else instructed him to change out of his suit and tie and redress in a white T-shirt and pants. After that, he joined others in line for the baptism. Candidates were submerged in the water by twos. Moments later, they reappeared, some were praising God; others seemed to be overcome with emotions.

When it was his turn, Daniel was told to cross his arms, then minister proclaimed, "My dear brother, upon the confession of your faith and the confidence we have in the blessed Word of God, concerning His death, burial, and Grand Resurrection, I now indeed baptize you in the only name under heaven whereby men must be saved, Jesus Christ, and God shall fill you with His Spirit, which is evidenced by speaking in unknown tongues."

The minister dunked Daniel under the water from head to toe and swiftly pulled him to his feet. The tears Daniel thought he had shed before was nothing compared to the ones streaming down his face now. Pumping his hands in the air, he shouted, "I'm free. I'm free." He practically leaped out the baptismal pool.

He didn't understand his out of control reaction. Before Daniel could examine it, a force so strong almost pushed him back into the water as he was climbing out. It was unexplainable as he listened to and felt his mouth move, uttering a language he had never learned…

As if he were a blind man, two other men had to lead him back to the changing room. He didn't realize that a towel had been draped on his shoulders until he was somewhat composed enough to dry himself off. Although he had control of his body as he redressed, his mouth was still spewing out phrases that he could only describe as heavenly.

Then his hands went up in the air again and his feet began to dance. There were others in the room under the same control. Daniel continued to speak until he ran out of steam. He lost track of time as he embraced the new spiritual experience. Eventually, he was guided back to the sanctuary where a few people still mingled.

Sitting in the nearest pew, Daniel closed his eyes and whispered his thanks to God for the indescribable experience. Just like the pastor had preached, Daniel did receive the Holy Ghost and had the evidence like a grocery store receipt in his pocket.

Daniel felt a shift on the pew and then a hand softly rubbing his back and singing softly. He recognized Saige's voice. Exhausted he sat back and opened his eyes. He expected to see her, but not her parents and cousins. How long had he been in the back and why were they there?

When he got to his feet, one by one, Saige's cousins pumped his hand and patted him on the back, but only her father explained what was happening.

"Congratulations, young man," Mr. Carter said. "When Saige sent us a video of you getting baptized, we rushed over. Salvation is a big deal, a tradition of sorts, to witness our family and friends' conversion."

Daniel didn't know how to respond. He knew the steps he took were life altering for him, but he didn't realize others would rejoice with him as well.

Her father continued, "It's nothing like laughing at the devil when God pulls you out of the fire from Satan's clutches. We're on the same team."

Saige's mother kissed his cheek and gave him a tight hug. Finally, Saige nudged the others out the way. She hugged him without saying a word. When she wouldn't release him, Daniel realized she was now crying.

"What's wrong, babe?" The endearment came naturally as he began to wipe away her tears when she looked up at him. Their relationship seemed to have been established before they met.

"I'm so happy for you." Saige hiccupped. "All you'll ever need is in Jesus." She hugged him again and lingered until her mother cleared her throat.

"Your cousins are gone, Saige, and we're heading out too." Mrs. Carter added, "Praise the Lord, Brother Daniel."

He nodded. "Thank you, Mrs. Carter, and yes, for the rest of my life I will praise God."

After they left, Daniel helped Saige into her coat and escorted her to her car. She didn't get in right away. "This means you're officially my brother in Christ."

The spiritual man in Daniel took a back seat in response to that statement. He looked at Saige in awe. "And, I'm officially your man—exclusively," he countered.

"I like the sound of that." Her lashes fluttered as her lips curved in a smile.

"I've never experienced anything like that in my life." He pointed to the church. "I'm not about to disappoint God or you." Opening her car door, Daniel patiently waited as she got in. "I've worked up an appetite. How about dinner?"

"Trail me home, I'll drop off my car, then I'll ride with you. We can decide on the way there."

She trusted him. Daniel blinked. He couldn't get to his vehicle fast enough to do just that.

Chapter 9

Daniel never had a desire to do drugs, but after Sunday's experience at church, he was riding high. Nothing seemed to faze him—nothing, and Jason took notice. His friend was the first of many people Daniel shared his testimony with after flowers arrived at the office.

The delivery man placed a medium-sized square box on Daniel's desk, then asked for a signature. The arrangement was more subtle with orange short stemmed roses and green carnations. Everything else was green plants.

"Well, I didn't send them," Jason joked.

"I've got an idea who did." Daniel plucked the card off the side of the box. Since Saige came into his life, he would never view a card the same again.

Opening up the mint green envelope, he slipped out the card. On the cover was an African-American man in a suit with his arms raised. Opening it, Daniel took his time to digest every word: *GREETINGS in the name of JESUS! There is nothing sexier than a man who loves God. Salvation wears better than a tailored suit. You gained so much strength when you surrendered to the Lord. May God bless you in your spiritual journey.* Those words were printed on the card, but in Saige's handwriting, she added, *Thank you for coming into my life and making me exclusively yours.*

He had just received his first Saige Carter greeting card. "Yeah."

Jason leaned on his desk. "You have it bad, man. I have to meet this woman who has you wrapped around her finger." Folding his arms, Jason grinned wickedly.

"You've got it wrong. Yes, Saige has my heart, but God has my soul now."

"Huh? What are you saying?" Jason frowned.

And that had been the open door for Daniel to give his friend a play-by-play on what happened to him at Saige's church. When he finished, all Jason could say was "wow," before he returned to his desk. When Daniel phoned Saige to thank her for the flowers, his call went straight to voice mail, so he texted his message.

He began to look forward to each day, believing that whatever crisis came his way, he could handle it. As a matter of fact, Daniel had even stopped obsessing over his family. He had turned that care over to God just like he had read in 1 Peter 5:7. As a result, God seemed to reward for the faith he was building in Him. Before the week had ended, he received a call from his mother in Detroit.

"Danny, thank you for sending me that nice card in the mail. It brought tears to my eyes. I've missed you, son. You hardly call anymore. I thought you had forgotten about me and your family." The relief in her voice made his old grudges seem so trivial now.

There were so many things Daniel wanted to say that he choked. He was no longer that same angry man he was the last time they had spoken. God had changed him. "I've never missed sending you checks twice a month."

"I get your daddy's pension and social security. I'm comfortable, but I'd rather see my son. You walked away and stayed away. Why?"

Surely his mother wasn't clueless. He was about to give her a laundry list of his complaints, but it seemed as if God took over his mouth again. This time plugging it.

Hold your peace, I will fight your battle, God whispered.

Daniel nodded as if Jesus was standing face-to-face. *God had His work cut out for Him,* he thought. *He* might have changed, but what about his family? Israel and Palestine had a better chance at signing a peace accord than the Washington's.

The doubt trying to come at him was counter-productive. "My reasons don't matter anymore. That was in the past..." *He hoped.*

"It's time you came for a visit. People change. I miss you," his mother paused with a longing in her voice that pricked his heart.

"I miss you, too, Mom." Daniel paused. "I'll be home for Christmas." He was about to share his salvation experience with his mother, but Eloise Washington became so excited, Daniel couldn't get a word in, so all he could do was laugh.

When his phone beeped, he expected it to be Saige. His little woman was working late at the university with holiday events. Instead, the call came from another Michigan area code. "Mom, I have another call—"

"Oh, it's probably your sister. When Phyllis got your card, she couldn't wait to call you, but I told her that I was doing it first. Talk to your sister, then call me back!" she demanded.

Chuckling, Daniel promised. Grinning, he hurriedly

said goodbye and answered the other line. "Hello?" He held his breath, hoping for a friendly discussion versus rehashing old arguments.

"What's going on, big brother?" Phyllis' voice was just as perky as his mother's had been. "Your card was so beautiful that I cried. I had been thinking about you—us— a lot lately. I know I said things that I shouldn't have, but I was angry that you were right," Phyllis rambled as if she was being timed to get it all out in one breath. Her apologies came with sniffles.

Daniel thought about the Scripture he had recently read about God making his enemies his footstool.

Your family is not your enemy, God whispered, correcting him.

It surely had seemed like it at times. Daniel gritted his teeth in annoyance at his flashbacks. He had to let the old wounds heal. While he was doing a self-analysis, his sister chatted away about the antics of her sons— she had one more now than she did when he moved away—and the long hours her husband, Lance, was working while going back to school. Phyllis had become a daycare provider, so she could be at home with the children and earn a little extra money. She didn't say it as if she was blaming him for her financial woes, but as if she was proud that she had found a way to rise above her circumstances.

Still, guilt touched his heart. With his means, Daniel should have been there for his family. "Well, sis. I plan to be home for Christmas."

"Yes! I can't wait to see you and introduce you to your new nephew. Wait until you see Ryan Daniel. He looks so much like you I gave him your middle name.

Daniel was honored. She didn't have to do that. Had

this division been one-sided all along? Phyllis hadn't mentioned their younger brother, but Daniel wanted to know. "What's going on with Thomas?"

At first, Phyllis was silent. It was like the motor in her mouth stalled. He braced himself for whatever she was about to say.

"He's out of control," she fussed. Personally, I think Mom's an enabler, but she says someone has to have faith in him to turn things around. You know Thomas—he has an attitude the size of the earth."

Some things never changed. Daniel shook his head, but he couldn't let that put a damper on his homecoming. Two out of three weren't bad odds. "Well, I'm looking forward to seeing everybody next month."

"I can't wait!" Phyllis screamed, forcing Daniel to put some distance between his ear and the phone.

"Me either."

Their twenty or thirty-minute call was cut short When Ryan and Lawrence had gotten into something that was about to land them in trouble. Daniel could only imagine their mischief. He chuckled, recalling the days when he and his younger siblings stayed in trouble. Those had been the innocent days of childhood, before adult disagreements separated families

"Love you."

"I love you too," he returned the affection, but it was too late. Phyllis had already disconnected their call. Smiling, Daniel wandered through his home and turned on a few lights. Next, he warmed up a slice of sweet potato pie that Mrs. Carter had sent home with him. A few hours later when he still hadn't heard from Thomas, Daniel debated if he should be the one to reach out to him.

If your brother trespasses against you, you extend the olive branch to gain your brother, God whispered Matthew 18:15.

"Lord, I'm not there yet." He wasn't prayed up enough to hold his tongue if his brother said the wrong thing. Taking a seat at the table to eat his pie, Daniel called his mother back. They spoke for hours, until his mother's favorite crime shows were about to start. Yes, some things never changed. He thought about what God had said. "Ah, is Thomas around?"

"No, son. I haven't seen Tommy since yesterday. I hope he's all right. You know the streets are dangerous and deadly."

"I'll pray for him. I love you, Mom." Daniel didn't move from his spot after they disconnected. God was truly turning things around in his life and it had begun only weeks ago while shopping for shaving cream. Who knew that a simple greeting card would take him down this road?

When his phone rang again, Daniel hoped it was Thomas. His disappointment was lessened when Saige's name flashed on the Caller ID. He barely told her hello. "They called, babe."

"Hallelujah," she rejoiced with him. "God told me His Word never returns back to Him without accomplishing what He sets out to do. It was meant for you and your family to reconcile."

Daniel grinned. Getting up, he walked into his bedroom and stretched out in the recliner near the large window. Staring outside, reminded him of Thanksgiving night, when he and Saige had gotten to know each other better.

"Unfortunately, it doesn't appear the card made any headway with my brother. Evidently, he hasn't changed."

"Maybe, because God hasn't knocked at his door yet. Let's pray that when his time comes, he'll be ready to open it. I'm so happy for you."

"Thanks. It feels good to have that connection again." he exhaled. "I'm going home for Christmas. I would like for you to go with me. All expenses paid and I'll put you up in the best hotel."

"Daniel," she said softly. "Holidays are meant to be with your loved ones. I don't want to miss a Christmas without my family, and neither should you. Go to yours and have a good time. I guarantee you won't even notice my absence."

"That is where you are wrong, Miss Carter. I believe you're the other half of my heart."

Chapter 10

Saige had never seen anything like it. As a shopper, Daniel was putting her to shame. The man was like a kid in a candy store, or a toy department. "For a person who hasn't celebrated Christmas in what, four years?" Saige stopped and smirked, "You shop like a pro."

"This coming from a woman who gets up before the sun to catch a five dollar sale," Daniel argued good-naturedly. They were pushing a cart together at a slow pace in a Toy R Us store.

"Just don't overdo it, okay? Didn't you say your generosity became a source of dependency on you?" she quizzed, leaning into him. Daniel put an arm around her waist while keeping one hand on the bar of the cart. She loved the small gestures of possessiveness. And with each touch, they were getting closer to that first kiss.

"Good point, but that was with my siblings. I have two nephews now. As an uncle, I have the God-given right to spoil them."

God knew Saige had no right to feel territorial, but she didn't want to share him with anyone else on Christmas. However, she wanted this happiness for him, but still... She looked up into his eyes and couldn't find the words to say how much she was going to miss him.

"What?" Daniel's stare drew her in. "Tell me."

"I'm going to miss you so much on Christmas." Her eyes teared as if he was going away to fight in a war or something. What a silly emotion.

"Hey." Daniel moved her and their cart to the side, out of the line of frenzied shoppers. "I'll call you with updates, and I won't stay long," his voice was soft and reassuring.

But to demand he follow through would be selfish—definitely a trait of being an only child. "No, I want you to re-acquaint yourself with your family and put me out of your mind while you're there. I want your family to be your focus, as mine will be this Christmas, and don't worry about me okay? Let's keep our talks and texts to a minimum."

A part of Saige wanted Daniel to protest—again an only child trait of wanting it to be all about her—but he hesitantly agreed.

They continued shopping until Daniel made her want to drop to the floor and not get up. Afterward, he made it up to her with a pedicure and, for kicks, he joined her. She got her nails painted in red-and-white stripes like a peppermint.

Daniel put a scowl on his face when the pedicurist came to him with clear polish. "Don't even think about it."

The technician nodded and hurried away.

Soon, it was the moment Daniel had been waiting for. His plane touched down at Detroit Metro Wayne County Airport. His excitement about coming home was being marred by the uncertainty of the reception from his brother. They had been extremely close and Daniel didn't like the void.

The what-ifs began to plague him. Despite the encouraging warm words from his mother and sister, he felt he was setting himself up to be trampled on.

Go in my name, Jesus spoke, *and all things will work together according to My purpose. Study Romans 8.*

Right. Daniel sighed as he walked off the plane and into the terminal. He noted the airport's renovations and the new shops that had taken up residence. With each step, Daniel debated what type of persona he wanted to display to his family—the confidence that he had at his firm or the humility that God required of him as one of His saints. Turning on his smart phone, Daniel grinned when he read Saige's text: *Don't let the devil steal your joy. You got this in Jesus' name. Be yourself.*

That woman was in tune with him, and that was why he was falling in love with her. He almost stumbled as he let the admission process in his head. Yes, he was attracted to her beauty, but Saige gave him something other women didn't—her. She was honest, open, and independent—not clingy, as some of the women he dated in the past had become.

Will do, he texted back as he rounded the corner and almost stumbled again. What was wrong with him? He knew how to walk, but it was what he saw that made him blink. A small group of hand-waving folks, some with balloons, were trying to get his attention.

He quickly did a head count: his mother, sister, her husband, and the two boys. Even a couple of his cousins were there. That was a surprise. Daniel wasn't expecting that. Grinning, he walked closer,—his younger brother was a no show.

Keep My joy. It is your strength, even in a storm, the Lord gave him a boost, leading him to Nehemiah 8.

They didn't wait for him to come to them. Instead they raced toward him with a force that almost knocked him over.

"Hey," Daniel appraised everyone. His mother had aged, but appeared to be healthy. His sister—wow, beautiful, even after two sons.

"This is your Uncle Danny, Ryan. Give him a hug," Phyllis said, but it appeared his nephew needed very little coaxing as he reached for Daniel.

Releasing his carry-on, Daniel lifted the sturdy child in his arms. The boy was friendly and squeezed his tiny arms around Daniel's neck. Daniel swallowed to keep his emotions in check as the love engulfed him. One by one, family members hugged him, including Phyllis' husband whom he had once threatened to make him respect his sister and be a man. It appeared Lance had done just that. Despite the joy, Thomas' absence felt like a sting. Could he and his brother mend the divide? He listened for God to answer—nothing. "I need to get my luggage from baggage check." They all started to walk in that direction.

"How long are you staying?" His first cousin, Jerome, asked. "Hopefully, we can catch up."

"Three days..." He grinned, "And even then, I don't know if I can stay away from my pretty lady that long." Daniel counted to three before the inquisition started.

"Am I about to have another daughter?" his mother asked.

"I'll finally have a sister!" Phyllis exclaimed as Daniel exchanged an amused look with her husband.

"Is she a girl, Uncle Danny?" Lawrence, the older of the two nephews, wanted to know.

"I'll tell you all about her when I get to the house. I see my luggage now." He pointed to the duffle bag filled with gifts for the boys and the suitcase that held more presents than clothes. He did listen to Saige though; he put a couple of items back, or he would have needed another bag.

Grabbing his things, everyone headed for the parking garage. Sitting between his nephews, one still in his car seat, Daniel relaxed in Phyllis' van, as Lance exited on I-94 Westbound toward Palmer Woods.

Yes, Detroit had taken an economic hit, but the Motor City was home. Yes, there were blighted areas, but there were also new developments since he was last there. But the GM Renaissance Center, Motown, and the world renowned Henry Ford Hospital would always remain landmarks.

As his sister chatted about the new Gateway Marketplace outdoor mall and some of the stores in it, Daniel's mind faded to the whereabouts of his brother and one of their many arguments. Then he stopped himself. No, he wasn't going to dwell on the past.

He had read Philippians 3:13 that morning: *but this one thing I do, forgetting those things which are behind, and reaching forth unto those things which are before.* When he had closed his Bible, he wondered if Jesus had directed him to that passage.

Lance turned off Woodward Avenue onto Seven Mile Road. It was the upper middle class neighborhood of doctors, lawyers, and teachers as residents of the almost three hundred spacious homes community. Yet, tucked away behind tall trees was a small Tudor house that had gone into foreclosure. Daniel was able to snag it at a great price for his mother. With Phyllis married and moved out, it was no wonder his mother wasn't eager to see Thomas leave the four bedroom home. Maybe, it was time for her to downsize. Stop it! There he went already, trying to run people's lives again.

The homes appeared professionally decorated for Christmas. When Lance pulled into the long driveway, his mother's house had been decorated as well. Had Thomas done it?

His mother looped her arm through Daniel's, slowing his steps to her front door. "I'm happy to have you back home. This will truly be a good Christmas. Now," she lowered her voice, "Thomas is a little down, because he got laid off again, so be nice to him."

Déjà vu. So he was still singing that song where most likely he was fired, but Daniel held his tongue.

"Don't go in there acting like the big brother. He needs a friend, especially with the baby coming."

"What baby?" Daniel froze and turned and squinted at his mother. "Your brother's girlfriend is pregnant. She's due around Valentine's Day." Eloise beamed.

There was so much wrong with this picture—no job, no wife, but a family coming

Hold your peace, God ordered.

Gritting his teeth, Daniel acknowledged the Lord's presence. It was harder to let go of the past than he thought. "Then I guess congratulations are in order."

His mother opened the door and walked in ahead of

Daniel. He stepped into the foyer behind her and breathed in the familiar surroundings. Except for a few new knickknacks, everything seemed the same. Instead of heading upstairs with his luggage to one of the guest bedrooms, his brother-in-law did it for him.

Wandering into the living room, Daniel was first surprised, and then not, to see his brother stretched across the sofa, watching a sports commentary show.

Thomas eyed Daniel, then went back to watching his program. His brother's rejection hurt. Did he purposely not go to the airport with the others?

Be the bigger person, he could hear Saige say.

Pride is destruction, God said loud and clear to his spirit. *Have you not read in 1 Timothy 6:4: He that is proud knows nothing? Strife of words brings about envy, strife, railings, evil surmising.*

His family seemed to become as an audience in the background as he stepped further into the room. Thomas hadn't made a move to greet him.

"It's good to see you, bro." Extending a hand, Daniel waited and hoped Thomas would at least shake it.

When his brother did reach for his hand, Daniel yanked him to his feet and locked him in a bear hug. "I'm sorry I stayed away."

Thomas said nothing in return and after a few moments, struggled to free himself from Daniel's stronghold.

"Yep." His brother was about to flop back on the spot he vacated when their mother fussed.

"Thomas! You can show your brother more love than that. He's been gone for four years," Eloise fussed as she removed her coat.

Was their mother calling them both out? "Not anymore, Mom. I'm coming home for Christmas and every holiday from now on."

"Money can't buy you love," Thomas mumbled under his breath.

Satan, you do not have the victory over this situation! Daniel silently prayed, refusing to take the devil's bait, even if he was using Thomas to deliver the blows.

Seemingly ignoring the tension, Phyllis, her family, and their two cousins gathered in the living room to catch up as Daniel settled into a recliner. Thomas remained on the sofa, but didn't add to the conversation. His mother beamed with pride holding Ryan, who had dozed off on her lap. Stretching out his legs, Daniel crossed his ankles. It felt good to be home.

When Daniel stifled a yawn, everyone announced it was time to leave. "Hey, I'm just a little jet lagged, you don't have to head off," he said to no avail as they left and his mother retired to bed. Suddenly, Daniel got a boost of energy. He wasn't sleepy or tired. Alone with his brother, he was ready to challenge Thomas to put every hurt and offense on the table for discussion.

But God whispered, *Hold your peace.*

He inwardly groaned, not wanting to. Daniel wanted a knock down drag out fight to resolve their differences, he knew that was his flesh talking, but God had already spoken, so Daniel got to his feet and stretched. "See you in the morning."

Thomas didn't say a word as he walked out the room.

Once Daniel was upstairs in the guest bedroom behind closed doors, he sat on the bed and bowed his head in prayer. "Jesus, you changed me. I was hoping You would have changed Thomas too. Why does he make me feel guilty?"

The devil is the accuser, not your brother, God answered, then referred him to Revelation 12:10.

Daniel appreciated that God was listening to his prayers and speaking to him throughout every interaction with his family. As he poured out his heart to Jesus to fix it, the Lord became his intercession through other tongues and Daniel stayed on his knees until his spirit quieted.

Then, he unpacked and prepared for bed. Even though he wasn't hyped about the commercial aspect of Christmas, he wouldn't mind Saige gift-wrapped under the tree in the morning. With a smile on his face, he drifted off to sleep with a silly notion that Santa Claus would grant him that wish.

Christmas morning, Daniel woke to little voices and coffee. Squinting, he noted the time on his phone and groaned. It was 8:00 a.m., which meant his body was still stuck on 7:00 a.m., St. Louis time.

He rolled over and hid under the covers, but soon louder voices mingled with the little voices, and whatever was under the tree had a sound of its own.

Getting up, Daniel slid to his knees to pray. He gave thanksgiving to see another day and his family, but he also prayed for guidance on how to handle his brother. Once he said Amen, he received a text from Saige.

Happy Jesus' birthday. I know you're glad you're home. I'm praying that it will be a good visit.

Instead of texting, he tapped her number. When she answered, Daniel greeted her with Merry Christmas. "Is it possible for me to want to be at two places at one time? I miss you."

"Yes, I miss you, too, but this is important, and I want your spirit to be at rest. Just follow where God leads."

"I will." Daniel wanted to stay on the phone, but she was getting ready for church service, which he wished he was there to attend.

Once the call ended, Daniel showered and dressed. By the time he went downstairs with an armload of gifts, the living room was trashed with discarded gift paper, empty boxes and toys galore. And there were still more to be opened. "Merry Christmas, everyone."

"Hi, Uncle Danny," his younger nephew waved, and then jumped up and dragged out a present for him to open.

Surprised, Daniel dropped his load to accept it, and then tore it open like a kid. Colorful sweaters, which were good quality, peeped out from under the tissue, but it was the necktie with "favorite uncle" that made him take a deep breath.

Besides toys, Daniel also handed out Visa gift cards to his siblings; including his brother-in-law. The tears in their eyes displayed their gratitude before they said a word. After receiving their hugs, Daniel headed for the kitchen in search of his mother...and brother.

"Good morning, Mom, and Merry Christmas." He knew she liked wholesome movies, so while he was shopping in the Hallmark stores for cards for Saige, he ended up purchasing four boxed sets for her. "Your present is under the tree." Kissing her cheek, he gathered his five-foot something mother in a hug. He held onto her, trying to store up enough hugs to last until his next visit. Closing his eyes he enjoyed the sanctuary of her closeness.

"I love you, too, son, but if I burn my bacon, I'll get a paddle to your behind." She laughed and Daniel released her.

Reaching into the cabinet, Daniel pulled out a mug for coffee and then fixed a plate of pancakes. At the table, he blessed his food and sampled the bacon. "Where's Thomas? He still does live here, right?"

Looking over her shoulder, she jutted her chin and squinted at him. "Yes, he does. Since he's not working again, he normally doesn't get up until about noon."

"Mmm-hmm." Daniel ordered his mind not to even go there.

"So tell me more about this incredible woman that had you grinning like an old man with new dentures last night."

"Saige is gorgeous and the sweetest person inside and out." He showed her a selfie of them on his smartphone." He couldn't help but grin, not concerned about the dentures remark. "This is Saige Carter. She's the one who penned the words in the card."

"And why didn't you bring her with you?" His mother gave him her full attention. "Then she really is someone special. That greeting card brought me to tears."

Daniel chuckled. "Yeah, she does have a way of humbling a person." He sipped his coffee. "Saige's praying for us to work out our differences and she didn't want to interfere. Plus, she wouldn't dare miss spending every holiday with her family."

His mother put a fist on her hip. "Of course, she would have to compromise when she marries you. I can tell listening to you that she's the one."

Did she just go there? Back one day and in his business, but there was no need for Daniel to deny his feelings. "She's very, very special and I miss her like crazy." Daniel grunted. "She also drew me to Christ. I got baptized in the name and with the Holy Ghost in Jesus name. Mom,

I would like us to have a family prayer today."

Eloise stared at him, then smiled. "That's just what we need – a family prayer. You lead it and I'll make sure the others join in."

Less than thirty minutes later, after everyone had eaten, except for Thomas, his mother announced a family prayer. "My prodigal son will lead us off."

Wow, did she have to call him that? Daniel cringed. "All right. Let's stand and hold hands." Phyllis, her husband, and sons did as she requested. Nobody mentioned Thomas' name.

Jesus, let this be about You, Daniel pleaded inwardly.

Forgive them, the Lord answered, *as I have forgiven you. Read My Word, Mark 11:26.*

"I want to say I'm sorry for saying or doing things that hurt anyone. I was hurt too, and I learned that I have to forgive others, whether a person asks for it or not. I want to be blameless when Jesus comes back." Closing his eyes, Daniel bowed his head. "Father, in the name of Jesus, we thank You for this day of celebration. I thank You for saving my soul and bringing me home. I praise Your name, because without You there is no healing. Thank You for the family that you've given me—and help us to love one another…"

By the time Daniel finished with Amen, everyone was either sniffing or had glossy eyes. Something told Daniel to glance behind him. Thomas was standing there, staring at him. His eyes were dry and his expression blank. Daniel could only hope that his brother heard some of the prayer.

Chapter 11

Saige couldn't stop thinking about her and Daniel's first kiss they shared when she dropped him off at the airport. It was tender and so sweet, but too brief. It was those memories that changed her Christmas. It just wasn't the same without Daniel. After celebrating their first Thanksgiving together, Saige wanted more time with him. But she knew he was winning over his family with his spiritual makeover.

However, she still had a Christmas to celebrate. She and Maxi attended their parents' church, Jesus is the Light Temple—another tradition. Her parents grew impatient as she hurried to finish dressing, then all three headed to service.

The church was packed as they joined the Winters in the pew. Saige and Maxi exchanged hugs. They had grown up in this church. As they got older, the friends switched their membership to Holiness in Jesus Temple, but always returned on Christmas to hear Pastor Evergreen preach the same Christmas message year after year. Yet, every time she heard it, it seemed like God gave her more revelation about who Jesus really was.

The worship was overpowering as the choir finished a soul stirring rendition of the Hallelujah Chorus. Finally, Pastor Arnie Evergreen stood at the podium and wished everyone a Merry Christmas.

"This is a great day," he started. "Whether the world wants to recognize Jesus' birthday or not, He's real. Isn't it wonderful that God's gifts aren't under a tree and we don't have to wait once a year to unwrap His blessing?"

"Amens" floated around Saige to mingle with hers.

"Yet, the downside is that not everybody knows who Jesus is. The Red Cross' motto is give the gift of life— donate blood. Christ has done that. He's given His blood for us to have eternal life."

Saige nudged Maxi and mumbled, "The Red Cross. That's a new angle. Good analogy." Her friend agreed.

Pastor Evergreen ended his sermon, reminding the congregation that one day can't do justice to show the greatness of Jesus' birth. "Now this is the portion of the service where you can be redeemed. The Bible says repent and be baptized. Do it today. Tell God you're sorry and be baptized to wash your sins away, then the Lord will give you the Holy Ghost."

When three men responded to his call to discipleship, Saige couldn't help but think about Daniel. She prayed that everything was working out the way he had hoped. At that moment, her mind was flooded with things he had said, done, or the way he looked at her. The scenarios were endless.

Maxi tapped her shoulder. "Get your mind off of Daniel," Maxi mumbled and giggled.

"Huh?" Saige blinked and glanced around. They had been dismissed? "What gave me away?"

"That goofy expression you get whenever you talk about him." She smirked and folded her arms.

"Okay, I'm not denying that I miss him. I wish he was here." Saige pouted and Maxi laughed as she gathered her things.

After warm hugs, Merry Christmases, and Praise the Lord's, the families said goodbye. It was Christmas as usual back at Saige's parents' house, opening presents, welcoming a steady stream of well-wishers, and gospel music playing throughout the house—and food. It was too much of it.

Despite all the buzz and good cheer of guests in and out of the house, Saige was lonely. After six weeks of dating, Saige craved her some Daniel Eggnog, Daniel pecan pie—Daniel anything.

Many hours later, the Carters had survived another festive Christmas. Her parents looked worn out. "Relax you two. I'll clean up," Sage offered. .

Once everything was restored, Saige strolled out of the kitchen. She smiled at the snapshot of her mother snuggling under her father's arm. They were staring into the fireplace. "Ah, lovebirds," Saige whispered. Married thirty-seven years, Adele and Richard Carter were inseparable. She wanted that same kind of happiness one day.

Exhausted, Saige was ready to retire to her old bedroom for another night there before going back to her apartment. She was halfway up the stairs when her parents called her. Turning around, she went back downstairs and stood in the doorway of the living room.

"I missed seeing Daniel today." Adele smiled. That wasn't the first time her mother had mentioned his name.

"Me too." Saige sighed and leaned against the door frame. "But I hope he's embracing the good and overlooking bad things with his family to have the happiness we have."

"I think he's good for you. He's confident—I like that about him, but he doesn't try to put on a front," her father said. "Surrendering to Jesus sealed the deal for me."

Saige beamed. "Thank you, Daddy." If any man wanted to be with her, he had to have her father's approval. Few made it to the second date, which accounted for her long droughts between dates.

"I hope he makes you happy." Her mother's voice was somber.

"He does." Saige frowned. She had already told her mother that. Walking further into the room, Saige flopped on the loveseat facing them. Their faces mirrored sadness as she looked from one to the other. "What's wrong?" Her heart took a nose dive. When they didn't answer, Saige asked again, "Mom, Dad, what's going on?"

"I hope you had a wonderful Christmas and always remember it." Adele swallowed.

"Of course I did. I loved the nostalgia tea set you gave me. It was beautiful. Now, we can have our own personal tea time." She chuckled, but her mother didn't. "Something doesn't feel right. We're having a conversation without anything being said." That was a phrase she could pen inside of a card for people who aren't communicating? *Who cares about cards right now,* she scolded herself. She felt like crying for no reason.

Her father cleared his throat and straightened his body without loosening his hold around her mother. "Well, this might be our last Christmas."

Before she reacted, she needed clarification. "What do you mean? Are you two finally deserting me for a vacation home in Arizona? Is that what this is all about?" Saige waved her hand in the air. "I have no problem celebrating Christmas without the snow."

Her mother leaned forward. "Saige Adele Carter, I have advanced stage ovarian cancer. It's inoperable."

Saige heard the words and watched her mother's lips move, but her brain was moving in slow motion and was unable to comprehend, then all of a sudden a force slammed into her chest and the understanding was immediate. "What!" She gasped as her vision blurred. Maybe something she ate was giving her this nightmare. But her mother and father's pain seemed so real. Saige heard herself ask, "When?"

"It was confirmed last week. We waited, because we didn't want to spoil your Christmas, but I didn't want to hold off any longer."

So many emotions raged inside Saige, she didn't know which one she would give permission to escape. "Well, my Christmas is spoiled. Cancer doesn't run in our family, so how…" Saige couldn't wrap her head around the diagnosis. "Mom, are you sure? Did you get a second, third, fourth opinion? Whatever it takes to prove the doctor wrong?" How dare the devil come into her life and tear her family apart?

"That was my third opinion, sweetie. Unless God intervenes, I'll make my transition…"

Covering her ears, Saige released her angst. Falling to her knees, she sobbed uncontrollably. This wasn't supposed to happen. Next year, she and her mom were supposed to start planning a fortieth wedding anniversary gala. Adele Carter was supposed to be a grandmother, the mother of the bride, the…. "No, this isn't supposed to happen."

Her father reached down and pulled her up beside him as if she was a little girl, which made her cry harder. Wiping at her tears, Saige looked into her mother's face.

"How long? How long do the doctors say you have...to...to live?" Uttering the words seemed to make it real, as tears continued to stream down her face as if she were releasing a gallon of water. The news was heart-wrenching. Saige was surprised the contents of her stomach remained in place.

"Ssh," her mother shushed Saige, rubbing her back.

"I told the doctor I don't want to know because life and death is in God's hands."

Her mother was too calm to be talking about her own death. Saige would be hysterical and whirling objects around the room. "The devil is a liar! I can't accept this. We have to pray that God will heal you. I have faith!"

Her father's sad eyes probably mirrored hers. "Unless God speaks a promise of life, we can't put faith in what He doesn't give us," he stated just as calmly as if he were okay with losing the love of his life. Both were too composed for her.

"We'll pray that God's will be done. Today's celebration is a reminder that Christ was born and died for a purpose—my salvation," her mother added.

Saige couldn't think about Christmas right now; she rubbed her temples to ward off a massive headache as her mother kept talking.

"Remember when I took you to see the Lion King on Broadway and the countless times we watched it on DVD?"

Her life was in turmoil and her mother wanted to talk about the Lion King? She was too exhausted to answer.

"Everyone looked up to Mufasa—he was strong and

fierce," her mother continued. "but that movie literally showed the circle of life. Mufasa had to make room for the next generation and Simba stepped up to the plate as the ruler to sire the next generation. I'm passing the torch to you for you to show the generations that follow how to live holy and walk in the footsteps of the Harrison women.

Not only did Saige not want that responsibility, she sure wasn't ready for it.

If in this life only you have hope in Christ, then you are of all men most miserable, God spoke through the wind, referring her to 1 Corinthians 15:19. *You celebrated My birth, which occurred thousands of years ago. Now celebrate My purpose to prepare a place for you. There is a place for the saints…*

As the Lord's voice faded away, Saige's mind went blank. Sparks ignited in the fireplace, the music played softly, but no more words were spoken. She needed eternity for her mother's life.

In a zombie-like fashion, Saige stood on wobbly legs. As if she were in a trance she kissed her father's head, then hugged her mother tightly and didn't let go.

"Everything will be all right. All things work together for the good of those who love the Lord and are called to His purpose," her mother mumbled in Saige's ear.

At the moment, the Scriptures couldn't penetrate her mind. It was bittersweet. Her Christmases would never, ever be the same again. She also never wanted to remember it—ever.

Chapter 12

God, I need more time, Daniel thought as he boarded the plane late, looking for an empty seat. Three days couldn't replace the years he had stayed away from Detroit, but he had done his best to squeeze in every minute with his family.

The smiles from his mother and sister made him feel like royalty. The attention from his nephews was indescribable, but it was the group hug on his mother's doorstep that meant the most, even if Daniel had initiated it with Thomas.

The love was so overwhelming, and his sister didn't want him to go, which was the reason why Daniel barely made his flight. Now, as he considered his seating choices, he eyed the two available middle seats. The women in both rows looked at him with a hopeful expression, as if saying, "you can sit by me."

Playing it safe, Daniel opted for a row with a mother and her toddler. Strapping in, he turned off his phone. He had planned to call Saige once he arrived at the airport, thinking he would have plenty of time as he waited for his flight. But, the phone call didn't happen.

One thing was for sure, Daniel wouldn't stay away from home so long again. Saige had been right. Holidays were meant to be shared with family. Maybe, she would visit with him the next time.

Although he and Thomas didn't have an honest man-to-man talk, Daniel overheard tidbits about Thomas' girlfriend. He was able to piece together enough information about when his future niece would arrive. It appeared Thomas was trying to make some changes. Before the baby came, he and Thomas *would* have that talk, and instead of automatically setting up a trust fund like he had done after Phyllis had Lawrence, Daniel would get Thomas's permission first.

Now that his mission with the Washingtons was a done deal, he could focus his attention elsewhere. *Saige.* He loved her and he planned to tell her that when she picked him up from the airport.

Glancing out the window, his mind stirred up the images it had captured a few days earlier when Saige dropped him off at Lambert Airport. Daniel hadn't meant for their first kiss to happen in an airport, but it had. Saige didn't seem to regret it either. Once he had cleared the security area and grabbed his keys and belt, she blew him an air kiss.

She was beautiful in her leather cap and sleeveless jacket. One thing he had grown accustom of was Saige's fondness for sweater dresses, tights and boots. Daniel had no complaints. He liked the hint of what God had hidden from every man.

"Would you like something to drink, sir," a flight attendant interrupted his musing.

Daniel declined. All he craved was another warm kiss

from Saige. He couldn't wait to hear about her holiday and share his.

The un-eventful two hour flight from Detroit to St. Louis seemed like four hours by the time his plane touched down in St. Louis.

Immediately, he turned on his phone and texted Saige.
Landed

Here.

That's all Daniel needed to know as he waited impatiently to grab his bag from the overhead storage before he exited the plane. Wouldn't he know it—his gate was at the end of the terminal. He took long strides to get to Saige.

He zoomed in on her in the midst of a crowd, looking for him, before she even saw him. His heart gave him a boost of energy. He walked toward her, a smile growing with each step until he invaded her space. Then he frowned. The light in her eyes was dimmed. Her readymade dazzling smile was missing. He hadn't been gone that long for the sad face. "Honey, I'm home." He grinned and opened his arms.

Saige fell into them and sobbed against his chest. Alarmed, Daniel dropped his carry on and tightened his hold. This definitely wasn't a "she missed me" cry. "Baby, what's wrong?"

A bystander nearby mumbled, "Young lovers. He must have been away a long time…"

Evidently so, Daniel thought, Or there was another reason for her anguish. "Hey, I'm here." He kissed the top of her head, then softly asked God to fix whatever was wrong.

He guided her to a less traveled area in the lobby of the airport. Next, he tried to guide her to a seat, but she wouldn't release him. Taking the seat himself, he lowered her on his lap.

"You have to talk to me, babe," he spoke in a soft voice.

A hiccup came out instead. Hugging her tight, Daniel resolved that he would have to be patient, something he hadn't mastered in his thirty-three years. He rocked her and cooed in the ear that he loved her—again not the perfect place, but it was the right time to let her know that whatever it was, she had his love.

Finally, Saige's sniffles ceased. "My mother is dying." Her voice was so faint, Daniel had to strain his hearing.

"What? What did you say?"

Saige repeated what he thought he had heard. "My mother has cancer. She...she might not be here next year." Saige hiccupped and started bawling again.

There had to be some mistake. Mrs. Carter was dying? "No." He shook his head in disbelief. Daniel felt like crying, but he had to be strong for her. Here was his little lady—his cheerleader for rebuilding his shaky relationship with his family for a Merry Christmas, while all the while her solid foundation was being shaken. Why couldn't their lives line up?

"I'm so sorry, babe. Why didn't you call me? I would have been on the next flight here."

"I didn't want to spoil your Christmas. You're still the first person I've told. Maxi doesn't even know yet," her voice choked as she looked up into his eyes. The sadness in her normally clear brown eyes twisted his heart. "I'm going to need strength to get through this. How can I celebrate my holidays—Christmas—without my mother?"

Daniel had no answer. His estrangement from his

family had been rough, but he had tried to keep up an indifferent facade until Saige came into his life. "And there's no cure, operation, or medicine?" He was grasping for any glimmer of hope.

Hope thou in God, the whisper came through the wind, but Daniel couldn't tell if God was asking a question or stating it. It was almost as baffling as Psalm 42:5 and Psalm 43:5, being almost identical.

He grabbed her hand. "Whatever you need— whatever—I'm here."

She nodded and then wiped at the tears that continued to leak from her pool of sorrow.

Hugging Saige, he let her cry as he tried to keep his own composure. His bags were probably circling on the carousel in the same way his emotions were spinning in his head.

Saige hadn't meant to fall apart in Daniel's arms, but she needed his strength. He told her he loved her, but she didn't have the strength to tell him back.

When her energy returned, Saige straightened her body on his lap and looked into his eyes that seemed to have absorbed some of her sadness. What a way to end the holidays.

Suddenly she became self-conscious about her appearance. Saige began to pat her face, but Daniel stopped her. "I know gentlemen are supposed to carry handkerchiefs, but I don't. Wait here." Gently picking her up, he placed her in the chair next to him, then Daniel stood and walked into the direction of the restroom.

Saige dropped her face into her hands. Daniel returned with dampened paper towels. He squatted in front of her and began to pat her face as if she were a little girl and he was making her presentable.

"I must look scary right now." She tried to joke.

"I happen to like scary right now." His intense stare indicated he wasn't joking.

"I love you too," her throat was so scratchy, it didn't sound sexy at all.

"I know." He leaned in and brushed his lips against hers.

Helping her to her feet, Daniel wrapped his arm around her and angled her body to lean on him. Although Saige didn't need his support, she needed his closeness. He picked up his carry on and, in unhurried steps, they made their way to the baggage claim to retrieve his items.

"Give me your keys," he demanded once he had his bags. She reached into her purse and handed them over without protest. "I don't like it that you were driving upset."

She had no comeback as she linked her fingers through his. Once they hit the cold air on the way to the parking garage, Saige felt she had actually depleted her reservoir of tears. "Tell me how your holiday went with your family. I need some good news." She desperately needed a diversion away from thoughts of her mother's impending death.

Daniel seemed hesitant at first, then he gave her a recap of some of the antics of his nephews and the scowl that his brother wore most of his visit. Saige smiled.

She felt the life coming back to her as she laughed. Everything about Daniel distracted her—his cologne, the tender way he looked at her, and his voice. She hadn't realized that when Daniel parked her car, they were in front of her parents' house, not his. Saige blinked, then frowned. "Why are we stopping here?"

"Because I want to see your mother and father." He made it sound like a statement, not a request.

Shaking her head, Saige tried to dissuade him. "You don't—"

He waved his hand before he unfastened her seatbelt and then his. "Why wouldn't I want to see them? Your parents have been very nice to me. We're in this together, Saige. When you hurt, I hurt, and I'm not happy until you're happy."

Once they were outside her car, Daniel took her hand in his. The short pathway to her parents' house from the curb was beginning to seem a mile long. Saige rung the bell to alert her parents she had company before inserting her house key in the door. Once her mother saw Daniel walk into the living room, her eyes lit up, even her father grinned and stood to offer Daniel a handshake.

"How was your family in Detroit?" her father asked.

"Wonderful, sir. I'm glad I went home, but…" Daniel stopped and removed his coat as if he planned to stay awhile. Then he helped to remove hers.

Taking her hand, Daniel let her sit first before he sat next to her. "But I'm shocked to hear about the news Saige has shared with me. Mr. and Mrs. Carter, I'm here for you and Saige. Please consider me as part of the family."

Saige didn't know where the water came from, but she suddenly burst out in tears. She was in Daniel's arms in seconds. His hush words were comforting, aiding her in composing herself.

She wiped at her tears, then Daniel pulled some tissue out of the box on the mantle. For the second time that night he patted her face dry as her parents looked on, amused despite the dark time in their lives.

I shall wipe away all tears from your eyes, God whispered. *There shall be no more death, neither sorrow, nor crying, neither shall there be any more pain: for the former things will pass away. You have My word on it. Revelation 21:4.*

While Daniel chatted with her parents, Saige meditated on what God told her. Daniel stayed awhile that night as if he didn't have to work the next day. When she yawned from exhaustion, her father offered to take Daniel home.

"'Night, baby. Get some rest. We need to send up a lot of prayers," Daniel said, then walked out the door.

A week later, Saige still hadn't accepted her mother's fate. Daniel came over to her parents' house with games and snacks and they celebrated the New Year as family, since she had no desire to go out. Maxi and her parents, Mrs. and Mr. Winters and Maxi, stopped by and took the news of her mother's illness just as hard.

As the weeks passed, Daniel was her lifeline, texting her prayers and Scriptures throughout the day. If he sent her flowers, her mother got them too. The days she spent the night at her parents', Daniel would stop by with meals for everyone or have something delivered. His thoughtfulness hadn't gone unnoticed by his father who sang Daniel's praises constantly.

Adele Carter's name was placed on numerous church prayer lists. Because of her grave prognosis of stage four cancer, her mother hadn't planned to undergo any kind of treatment, but Saige begged her, "Mom, please. Let's try everything until God says something different." So her mother consented.

What Saige hadn't expected was for Daniel to take off work early the day her mother started her chemotherapy. He was there for her.

"Promise me that if Daniel asks you to marry him, you'll say yes," Adele whispered with tears in her eyes as they sat in the treatment, waiting for her turn.

"I will, Momma." She grabbed her mother's hand and squeezed it.

"Only if you love him," her father added, sitting on the other side of the bed. "Still, he better talk to me first."

She and her mother exchanged smiles.

"I will, sir," Daniel said, coming in the room with cups of hot chocolate from the cafeteria.

Saige blushed when Daniel winked at her. That put an end to any further discussion of wedding bells that day.

Chapter 13

"My mother's dying?" Even though she said it, she couldn't comprehend what that meant. "Not if God intervenes. Maybe, it's only a test." Maxi's attempt at encouragement was falling on deaf ears.

To cheer her up, Maxi had demanded Saige leave her apartment to window shop in the greeting card aisles at different stores. The excursion usually made Saige forget her troubles, but not today.

Saige went through the motions of admiring cards, but her heart wasn't in it and Maxi could tell. "This is hard, waiting for someone to die, not knowing if this day will be their last day, or next week." She didn't want to talk about death, but on the other hand, she needed to.

Maxi put her arm around her shoulder and squeezed it. "Come on, let's get out of here and hang out at your mom's."

Nodding, Saige sniffed and followed her friend out to the car. She couldn't get enough of seeing her mother right now for any excuse or any given day.

Thirty minutes later, they arrived at her parents' house.

Adele Carter was smiling and welcoming. As long as her mother looked happy and healthy, Saige was fine, but on the days she looked pale, Saige's mood soured.

"We're just about to play Monopoly. We could use two more players," she said in a hopeful manner.

Silently groaning, Saige wanted to back out. It wasn't that she didn't like board games, but there was usually an end to them within an hour or so. If memory served her correctly, Monopoly could go on for days. She was about to suggest another game when Maxi shoved her and frowned, then turned to her mother.

"Sure, Mrs. Carter. We have nothing else to do."

Actually, Saige did have stuff to do, like work on her next batch of greeting cards, but she had yet to do it.

Before the night was over, she and Maxi had fallen asleep at her parents' house like old times when they were teenagers. They parted ways the next day with tight hugs.

"You have no idea how much it means to me to call you my friend," Saige said with tears in her eyes. She didn't recall ever crying so much in her life.

"You would do the same for me, if it were my Mom. Besides, we're sisters and we stick together." Maxi gave her another tight hug, then left.

Nothing was routine in the weeks that followed for Saige and her family. And Daniel took notice and stepped in to make sure she took care of herself.

Although it had been a crazy past couple of days for Daniel at work, he showed up at her doorstep each evening with food in one hand and his laptop in the other.

Some days, it seemed like he forced fed her, not physically, but by the gentle persuasion of his words. "Eat, babe. I waited at Boston Market for hot sweet potatoes just for you." It was his patience that coaxed her to eat, then without realizing it, she had cleaned her plate.

Afterward, Daniel would clean up their mess and power up his laptop. Saige would snuggle up next to him. She felt safe, loved, and blessed with him in her life. They had become so comfortable in the routine that Saige didn't realize she was mimicking her mom and dad.

For three evenings in a row, Daniel powered up his computer and she snuggled next to him. "I haven't seen you work on any cards lately," he said while reviewing a document.

Saige shrugged. "No inspiration." The company paid her on consignment anyway. She already had a day job, so she wouldn't starve. "I don't know if I ever will again." She didn't want to talk. All Saige wanted was to listen to him tap on the keys and, at times, mumble to himself.

The muscles in Daniel's shoulder where she was resting her head, flexed, then he pushed his computer to the side on the table and faced her. "Your love inspires me, and I had hoped that my love did the same for you," he said softly. He kissed her with such tenderness that Saige had to reconsider her thinking.

He pulled back and Saige pouted.

"It's been a while since you've shown me anything you've worked on. Get your computer," he ordered softly. "Please."

Getting up to do his bidding, Saige hoped he was not about to force her to start writing. He would be wasting his time and hers. Her heart was hollow. Swiping her home computer out of her makeshift corner home office, Saige returned and placed it in from of him.

She turned it on per his request and folded her arms.

He seemed at home, opening up her graphic design program. Then she watched in awe as he breezed through the navigation.

Looking up at her, Daniel winked. "Once you design with CAD, this is a piece of cake." He chose a design in Photoshop, then altered it in Adobe Illustrator. The image wasn't as elaborate as she would have made it, but his message made her smile.

I don't need a Valentine's Day card to tell the woman who captured my heart that I love her. She already knows, but these words only serve as a record that I love you. I want all your senses to feel my love when I touch your lips, see you looking at me in a way that only you can to make me smile, and hear you whisper your love back, I get inspired to be the best man I can be for you. With all my love, Daniel.

Here I go again. Saige swallowed to rein in another crying binge, but this time they were happy tears. When he stood, she threw herself in his arms. She thought she would be boo-hooing by now, but she didn't. Saige felt content.

"That was so romantic. I love you too," she whispered and inhaled his cologne before stepping back.

"I wish I had been just as romantic when we shared our first kiss and telling you I loved you."

Lord, thank You for giving me this man. Saige rubbed his jaw. "You made it perfect. I love you, so much."

"I know." He winked. "Now, get to work. You need to inspire others. Plus, you said your mother had a good day. That's inspiring."

When her mother had good days, one of the church members picked her up and drove her to church for noon prayer. "There's comfort in being around the saints and on one accord," she often said. A few times, Saige had driven across town during an extended lunch break to pray with her mother.

"Yes, it is." Now, it was on. Nudging Daniel with her hips, Saige sat up and regrouped. The expressions seemed to ooze out of her heart: humorous, sweet, serious...whatever God gave her she wrote it.

The following weeks seemed to be kind to her mother as Saige, Daniel, and her father maintained a once a week fast and prayer day. The doctors said the chemo had slowed the spread, but the fact remained that her mother still had cancer, and God hadn't spoken a word concerning her healing.

Soon, Daniel's evening visits to her apartment slowed. The phone calls, cards, flowers, and occasional dinner delivery were all reminders that he was still thinking about her.

One morning, Daniel called before her alarm clock sounded. "Sorry, if I woke you, baby, but I need a yes or no, if you want your man to take the love of his life out for our first Valentine's Day. If I wait any longer, I won't be able to get reservations, even at White Castles."

She chuckled. It was no joke that even the ninety-something-year-old drive-through fast food joint transformed its White Castle image to a "Love Castle" on Valentine's Day. Workers dressed its small dining area with red tablecloths, candle lights, and floral centerpieces. Amazingly, reservations were hard to come by, whether couples were senior citizens or seniors in high school.

Saige just wasn't in the mood for a whole deal dress up affair. "You won't be upset if I say I'd rather stay in and celebrate just the two of us, will you?" She knew she wasn't being a very good girlfriend, but some days when her mother wasn't having a good day, Saige felt she had nothing inside to give Daniel. More than once she questioned whether if the timing of their meeting was off.

If Daniel was disappointed, he hid it well. "Then don't dress up. You're beautiful with or without makeup, in jeans or a dress. But I *have* to take you out. Ours mothers would think I'm less of a gentleman."

Since returning from Detroit, Daniel talked with his mother as if time had never separated them. Eloise always asked about her and her mother. "You have a point." Saige smiled. "But nothing fancy. Low key, okay?"

"Nothing fancy," Daniel agreed, and then in what had become a routine between them, he prayed before ending their call. "Lord, in the mighty name of Jesus, thank You for bringing Saige into my life. We thank You for the blood You shed on Calvary. Lord, let Your perfect will be done in our lives and those of our families. We ask thank You for giving Mrs. Carter grace and mercy, and if it be Your will, perform a healing in Jesus' name. Amen."

"A...amen." Saige mumbled as tears blurred her vision. She never knew how much she loved to hear a man pray until after Daniel surrendered his life to Christ.

"Okay, throw me my kisses, woman," he demanded. She obliged him with ear-piercing smacks on the phone. Laughing, she hung up, in a good mood to start her day.

"She's not cooperating," Daniel complained to his mother during one of their bi-weekly calls they began to exchange following his Christmas visit home. Actually, it felt good to have his mother guide him during this difficult time in his relationship with Saige who meant everything to him.

"Son, you're going to have to make an adjustment. Right now, it's all about her. The poor girl. It's hard to be happy when you know a loved one is dying. I know." Daniel knew that his mother was thinking about the death of his father. "But I don't know what woman wouldn't want to be pampered on Valentine's Day. It's up to you to be creative if you plan to propose."

Daniel couldn't wait any longer to ask Saige to be his wife. He had been ready the day he returned from Detroit. Once he learned about Mrs. Carter, he put his wants on hold to be there for Saige as she weathered the storm, which unless the Lord intervened, would only get rougher. "I'll work something out."

"You better, because Saige has made you a better man and I can't wait to meet her in person." Eloise disconnected.

It was time for Daniel to head home anyway. He hadn't seen a flaw in his design for the middle school proposal, but his boss had. Maybe after a good night's rest with a clear head, he would be able to pinpoint the problem. Before he got into his car, Saige texted him.

I'm sorry about my bummed out mood lately. Plan the night away.

"Yes! Let the love fest begin." Finally, Daniel would be able to pamper Saige like crazy.

Chapter 14

Daniel had outdone himself with the red rose arrangement he had delivered to her job for Valentine's Day. Come to find out, he had sent flowers to her mother too.

"You've got a jewel," her mother chatted away. The chemo had left her weak for a couple of days, but she seemed to be bouncing back. "Have you decided on what you're you wearing tonight? How about that red dress you wore…" the woman was practically dressing her from afar as if it was prom night. Saige wasn't complaining. She liked to hear the excitement in her mother's voice.

"And make sure you and Daniel stop by, so I can take a look…"

"Yes, Mother."

Saige wasn't getting any work done that day, because as soon as she said goodbye to her mother, Maxi called.

"Unless Daniel is taking you out for lunch or dinner, let's meet at your favorite place."

"See you in an hour." Saige disconnected and tried to answer emails. At least Saige was only minutes away from Boston Market.

The two arrived almost at the same time. They placed their orders, then found a table.

"So, do you know where Daniel is taking you?" Maxi's eyes were bright.

"I have no idea, but I'm glad I didn't talk him out of it." Love was in the air throughout her department. The candy, the stuffed animals, and the flowers added to Saige's excitement.

"Girl, I'd have disowned you as my friend if you had done that!" Maxi slipped out of her jacket, then flopped in her seat. "If only *I* could find the right one. Maybe I need to stake out somewhere with a sign that says, 'I'm available'."

"You are too silly." Saige laughed. "You know, when I was creating those greeting cards, I had no idea that I would meet a man so loving and sensitive."

"True, but he did have issues at first," Maxi reminded her as their plates were placed in front of them.

Once they blessed their food, Saige sampled the sweet potatoes and wasn't disappointed. "He did, but what makes him so strong and sexy to me was his vulnerability as he worked through them."

Maxi leaned closer and grinned. "So do you think he's going to propose? It is the day for lovers."

Was her friend actually holding her breath? Saige frowned and shook her head. "Hmm... I hope not. I mean, I love him. My parents love him. But the timing is off. I've been trying to cram in as much time with Mom as I can while she's still feeling good."

For the next few minutes, they ate in silence until Maxi sighed. "I still can't believe it—cancer. I know paradise awaits the saints in the Lord when we die, it's just the process of dying that I wish we could skip."

"And just think, Jesus didn't come down from the cross. The Lord is the God of testimonies. I'm praying that He will give Mom one."

"Amen."

With lunch finished, they stood and said their goodbyes. When Saige was in her car and about to drive off, she heard the Voice of God.

Your mother does have the testimony," He whispered. *She has overcome by My blood. She doesn't love this life more than dying in Me, so she can take part in the Resurrection.*

Holding her breath, Saige stared through the window shield. Tears blurred her eyes as she replayed the message from the Lord. She knew some of what the Lord said could be found in Revelation 12. As the first tear fell, Saige realized that was the closest answer she had received from God. In other words, He wasn't going to heal her.

She sat in her car for a good fifteen minutes and cried. There was no way she could return to work with her eyes puffy and face swollen. Saige called her mother, even though she had spoken with her only hours ago. "How are you feeling?"

"A little tired. Chemo is brutal," her voice faded.

She did not sound like the same perky woman from earlier. "I love you. Get some rest." Saige hurried off the phone before she started another bawling binge.

Once she had composed herself, Saige punched in her supervisor's number and requested the rest of the afternoon off and drove to her place. She wasn't ready to accept that her mother's days were truly numbered.

Daniel called a few hours later. "Hey, my Valentine, are you able to get off work early?" He sounded so excited.

"Yeah. I left after lunch." Saige's mind was drained from thinking about the Lord's words.

"What's wrong, baby?" The alarm was building in his voice. "Is your mother… all right?"

Saige shook her head at first. "No," she whispered. "She's dying."

The line was quiet. Finally, Daniel cleared his throat. "Honey, we know that."

"But God spoke to me," she repeated His message. "We've been praying for an answer and now that I have one, I don't like it. So you think Momma knows?"

"Probably, I don't think God would tell you without telling her, babe."

His words had such a calming effect on her spirit. While Jesus was preparing to take her mother away from her, He had given her a wonderful man to gather strength from.

"Life has to go on…and I'm here," Daniel said softly. "Get dressed. We're going out to a new place that I found last week. It's not the tux and formal attire atmosphere I had hoped, but I'm surer now that you will love it."

Taking a deep breath, Saige smiled. "Okay, how should I dress?"

"Wear that red dress you bought when I went shopping with you and make sure you bring your red lipstick."

That was an odd one. Saige's interest was piqued. "Why?"

"So I can kiss it off. See you in a few." He ended the call.

Giggling, Saige's spirits were lifted. She jumped into the shower, applied her makeup to perfection, including her lips, then slipped into the form fitting dress Daniel had alluded to.

At exactly six o'clock, she opened the door to see her tall, dark, and very handsome date.

"Wow, memory doesn't do justice of your beauty. You look gorgeous!" Stepping inside, he towered over her and barely brushed his lips against hers in a kiss.

Saige pouted. "You mean I put on this lipstick for that?"

"Later, let's go." He reached for her faux fur coat and helped her in it.

Daniel was quiet as Saige took in the scenery going away from North County. They bypassed the exit to the upscale restaurants in Clayton and West County. She frowned. "Are we going downtown?" Although she was dressed warmly, she had on four inch heels, which meant they were all show and not for walking downtown, especially on the cobblestone on Laclede's Landing. When Daniel turned off I-40 on Hampton Avenue, Saige was confused.

"I know that brilliant mind of yours wants to ask." Daniel chuckled and squeezed her hand. "But this is the best I could do with late notice."

She turned from looking out the window and faced him. "You always give me your best without trying."

Lifting her hand to his lips, Daniel rewarded her with a kiss.

Soon, he parked in front of Mike Talayna's Juke Box restaurant in the Dogtown neighborhood of South St. Louis City. The entrance was unassuming and gave little hint of any expectations. Once inside, it was like stepping back in time to a disco tech with its large disco balls and mirrored walls.

"Cute." She gave Daniel a dazzling smile. This was definitely something different. "How did you find this place?"

"I passed it on my way to a construction site. I was getting bummed out because I couldn't get into the places where I wanted to take you. For some reason, I came inside to grab a bite to eat and was blown away. The menu is limited to pizza, wings, and snack food, but I think the entertainment will serve the purpose."

Turning in his arms, Saige hugged him tight. "Although I feel a little overdressed, I like the atmosphere."

It didn't take long before Saige started enjoying herself. Some of the karaoke singers weren't bad, while others were hilarious. And Daniel was right, the wings were delicious. Saige didn't think anything of Daniel's absence when he excused himself to go the restroom. What did surprise her was five minutes later when she looked up and saw him on stage with the microphone.

Can he sing—really? Congregation songs didn't count. But with his rich baritone voice, if he could hold a note every woman in the place would be salivating after him.

When Daniel spoke into the microphone, it screamed a high pitch until the volume was adjusted. "Happy Valentine's Day to all the ladies, and especially to the woman I fell for the first time I looked into her beautiful brown eyes, Saige Carter."

Her heart fluttered. Something about his open declaration was embarrassing and exhilarating,

"Saige, will you stand?"

As she got to her feet, all eyes were on her, and that's when the embarrassment kicked in.

"When I first heard *'Someone to Love You'* by Ruff

Endz, I thought about you." From the moment Daniel sung the first line, every word revealed his passion, then she noticed he wasn't reading from the karaoke screen.

He knows the words? She sucked in her breath. At that moment, the crowd faded and time froze. Saige locked eyes with him. As the song ended, he reached out his arm and beckoned her to come to him.

As if in a trance, Saige obeyed until she was within kissing range. Watching Daniel get down on one knee, she faintly recalled her mother's words, "If he asks you to marry him…" At that moment, she realized that the timing couldn't be better. "Yes, Daniel Washington, I'll marry you."

Saige didn't know what he did with the microphone, because suddenly his hands were free as he wrapped his arms around her and lifted her off the floor.

It wasn't Daniel who kissed the lipstick off her lips. It was she who smeared it on his mouth, jaws, and nose in jubilation.

Chapter 15

"I can't believe you asked me to marry you! It was so romantic. I can't believe you could sing like that! I didn't want to take my ring off…"

Daniel could barely keep a steady hand to stroke the shaving cream off his jaw. He couldn't stop laughing at the high-pitched voice of his new fiancée screaming her elation through the speaker phone. If he had known Saige would be this ecstatic about wanting to be his wife, Daniel would have asked her sooner. It felt so good to hear her so happy.

Ouch. He nicked himself when Saige released another crazy scream. He may need a hearing aide before their conversation was over.

"I can't wait to show Mom my ring!"

Mrs. Carter. Daniel hoped and prayed that his future mother-in-law was having a better day than she had yesterday evening. "If I can get through shaving without using an entire box of Band-Aids, I'll be there as soon as I can get dressed to take my sweetheart out to breakfast."

Less than an hour later, the couple was dining at First Watch Café. The glow on Saige's face was enchanting. She had energy Daniel never recalled seeing before. It was downright comical to watch her attempts at trying to contain her excitement. A couple of times, he caught her staring at the 24K white gold diamond ring, then wave her left hand in the air when she talked to see the sunrays bounce off the diamond..

They had been so distracted with the thought of being engaged last night that the crowd at the restaurant cheered him on to put the ring on her finger.

"What?" Saige tilted her head, quizzing him.

So this is what it felt like to be in love. "I am one blessed man. This incredibly beautiful woman sitting across from me agreed to be my wife."

"Did you think I would say no?" Saige stole a piece of his turkey sausage. "I'm just praying that Momma will be alive to see us get married."

Daniel hoped so, too, because he knew that would make his wife-to-be happy. "The doctors still haven't said how long she has left?"

As Saige shook her head, the curls swayed from side to side. "She told the doctor she doesn't want to know and not to tell any of us, because God gave her the breath of life and He will be the One to take it away." She became quiet as if some of the joy was beginning to seep out. "What do you think about us getting married next month?"

Daniel choked on his juice. He reached for a napkin. Once he swallowed, he stared at Saige. "Baby, this isn't a shotgun wedding. It doesn't have to be a grand gala affair, but I don't want to go to a courthouse either. Let's give ourselves two or three months to make it special."

Saige glanced away and mumbled, "Can Mom last that long?" Before he could respond, she looked at him with a seemingly new resolve. "Okay. I always wanted to be a June bride, so I could have a garden wedding."

He reached across the table and placed his hand on top of hers. "I love you."

"I know."

Lord, help us—please. Daniel kept changing the subject until he could visually see the glow returning.

Once they finished eating or gazing at each other, Daniel drove them to Saige's parents' house. When they strolled through the front door, the scent of apple cider greeted them.

"Mom, Dad?" Saige called out.

"We're in the kitchen," her father answered.

With their hands linked and wearing big smiles, they turned the corner. Daniel tried not to stare, but since his last visit, Mrs. Carter had lost weight. Despite her weakness, she *ooh*ed and *ahh*ed over Saige's ring.

Mr. Carter had given his blessings more than a month earlier. "Good choice." Her father slapped him on the back and congratulated him. "In lieu of sparkling grape juice, how about we celebrate with a mug of apple cider?"

"I'm surprised the scent doesn't bother mom," Saige said.

Her mother patted the front of her sweater. Aside from the weight loss, she looked her normal self with her thin hair brushed back. "It's the only thing that seems to calm my stomach and that I can keep down."

Removing their coats, he and Saige joined them at the table. Saige recapped the previous night's event, leading up to his proposal. "I couldn't believe Daniel could sing like that and…" she elbowed him.

When it appeared that exhaustion was overtaking Mrs. Carter, she stood with the assistance of her husband and waved them back to her bedroom on the first floor. The master bedroom was tidy except for the bottles of medicine on a side table. With assistance from Saige's father, Mrs. Carter stretched out on top of the bedspread.

"Maybe we should go," Daniel whispered, standing in the doorway.

"No, just sit and talk. I want to hear about your wedding plans," Mrs. Carter said in a tired breath.

Daniel looked to Saige to decide. When his fiancée got comfortable in a chair, so did he in another. He patiently listened as Saige indulged her mother about wedding dress styles, shoes, cake, a venue, and on and on. She paused when they heard a light snore coming from her mother.

Mr. Carter nodded for them to go ahead and leave. Daniel was almost out the room when Mrs. Carter whispered his name. He went back to her and squatted by the bed as Saige and her father talked, going toward the kitchen. Her eyes were still closed.

"Thank you for loving my daughter and giving her something to look forward to in life."

Daniel blinked. He didn't know what to say. Daniel should be the one thanking her for giving him a special woman in his life. "That has been one of the easiest things to do."

He didn't know if she heard him or not because the faint snore returned. Getting to his feet, Daniel walked to the door, but glanced back at Mrs. Carter. He agreed with Saige. They *had* to move the wedding day up and pray that her mother would be alive to see it.

The next day after church, Daniel mentioned that to Saige while they were enjoying brunch at Wildflowers again.

"Are you sure?" She seemed confused by his reversal. Twisting her lips, Saige seemed to give it some thought. "Next month is out. Easter is early April this year. How about the first Saturday in May?"

"We'll make it work. Plus, our family and friends that will help—Maxi, my mother, Phyllis... We also need to schedule a counseling session with Pastor Hogan." he suggested.

"Of course, Maxi will be my maid of honor. Hopefully, Phyllis wouldn't mind being my matron of honor," Saige said, entering notes on her smartphone.

"She won't," Daniel was sure of it. "My nephew can be the ring bearer."

"Check." What about your best man?" she asked.

"Jason will be my groomsmen." Although his relationship with Thomas was weak, there was no one else who Daniel could think of to stand by him. "My brother will be my best man."

Chapter 16

"I know God is righteous." Saige paused to fight back tears as she and her mother—mostly Saige—composed a guest list for the wedding. They were sitting in the dining room perusing invitation samples that Saige could create herself in her graphic design program.

"And He is…" Adele's voice was weak from enduring another treatment.

"I wish we had more time," Saige paused. She meant for time in life. "You know to shop, prepare, and especially help me pick out my wedding dress."

"We still can." Adele reached out and touched Saige's hand. "We can shop online. I'm looking forward to being in the presence of the Lord. I've lived the time God gave me to reach my fullness in holiness, so there is no reason to have sorrow for me. It's the sinners who you need to mourn and pray for. I might not make it to sixty, but some people don't make it past twenty or thirty or forty. My life should be a celebration, so let's celebrate." The smile her mother mustered was next to glorious.

How could Saige be sad hearing such a testimony? "You're right. I can do the list later. Let's find me a dress!"

Saige got up and pulled out her iPad tablet from her purse. Together they viewed website after website. The task seemed to give her mother energy for hours before they narrowed down the choices to three.

Daniel called to check on her and that was the only break Saige took from the wedding preparations with her mother. Her mother had been right about internet shopping. It was just as exciting. She called Phyllis and put her on speaker phone. Her future sister-in-law suggested creating a board on Pinterest to pin pictures of wedding cakes and other unique ideas.

"Excellent," her mother loved the idea.

Finally, when it got late, Saige called it a night, but her mother seemed to be wide awake.

By mid-March, the plans were coming together. Her mother's health appeared to be stable—no worse or better. Everything seemed under control – her and Daniel's jobs started to demand more of their time.

When the owners of a new hotel project requested changes to the floor plan, Daniel had begun to work late to keep the completion date on schedule. Despite the demands, he never backed down on his share of the responsibilities for the wedding preparations.

But Saige got behind on submitting more seasonal greeting cards samples. And for some reason, instead of the witty, whimsical cards her publisher commissioned her to create, the owner felt her niche was soul-stirring cards for uncomfortable situations, maybe like the one she was going through now.

Frustrated, Saige opened her Bible. She hadn't been the same since the Lord sent His Word, concerning her mother's health. Saige no longer prayed for healing.

Comfort for her mother was now her prayer request. But the question always in the back of her mind was how long would the Lord allow her to suffer in this condition?

I am the resurrection, and the life: he that believeth in me, though he were dead, yet shall he live. And whosoever liveth and believeth in me shall never die. Believest thou this? God whispered as if He was quizzing her.

She knew God was referencing the eleventh chapter in John about Lazarus' resurrection.

Believest thou Me? God repeated, making no mistake that the question was for her, not Martha, Lazarus' sister.

"Yes, Lord," she whispered, bowing her head in shame. "I need You to help my unbelief that keeps popping up." A tear fell down her cheek.

I sacrificed My life, so the world wouldn't have to. Your mother is one of Mine. In no way will I cast her out.

Almost instantly, Saige began to regain strength in her spirit. God was indeed removing the unbelief. With renewed inspiration, Saige signed into her computer and began to create cards to celebrate the Resurrection, not Easter. It was as if God took control of her fingers on the keyboard just as He took control of her tongue when He filled her with the Holy Ghost.

Do you believe in Me?

My yoke is easy, My burden light. Rejoice in My Resurrection, Matthew 11:30.

My Resurrection is My love for the world.

I did it. I died for you!

She stared at the phrases she penned under the anointing of the Holy Ghost. When Daniel called, Saige took a breather. She couldn't believe God had given her 35 phrases for greeting cards. She smiled.

"Hi, baby, what ya doin?" he asked playfully. Tiredness was evident in his voice.

"Oh, working for the Lord." She filled him in on what God had said to her and what she had done with what to write.

"I'm so glad Jesus is giving you comfort through this process."

"Me too." Saige agreed. "I needed to hear a word from Him, because I got tired of my faith slipping, but the Lord has renewed my strength."

"And they shall mount up with wings as eagles. They shall run, and not be weary; and they shall walk…"

"And not faint," they said in unison the rest of Isaiah 40:31.

Chapter 17

The day had come, and Daniel had never seen a beautiful woman look more stunning than his bride, gliding toward him at the altar. Her brown skin glowed against the shimmering yards of lace and tulle. It was only right she had donned a rhinestone tiara that tangled in her mass of long curls. She was moments away from being his.

He followed the direction of Saige's eyes as she glanced at her mother, sitting regally on the front row. Daniel lifted a prayer of thanks for allowing Mrs. Carter to see this day—his and Saige's nuptials.

Mrs. Carter beamed as she dabbed her eyes. For a terminally ill cancer patient she looked rather well. The wig, makeup, and fitted evening gown gave no hint of her condition.

Moments earlier, Mr. Carter had slowly and patiently escorted his wife halfway down the aisle for pictures' sake. After numerous flashes, he had lovingly assisted her into a wheelchair. With pride, he wheeled her to the front.

Till death do us part, Daniel thought, then returned his focus to the love of his life so that he, too, could pledge

Saige until death do they part.

Daniel's best man on his left side cleared his throat. "Would you stop lusting at her, man? You're about to break out in a sweat," Thomas ribbed him.

Thankfulness swelled up within Daniel. It wouldn't be a grand affair without his family from Detroit. His oldest nephew had been the ring bearer, while a little cousin of Saige's served as the flower girl.

Forgiving had come easy for his mother and Phyllis. His younger brother was the hold out until the last day to order tuxes, which Daniel offered to pay for, but surprisingly Thomas said, "I got this."

So Thomas' off-handed remark was his subtle way of communication. Daniel would take it for now, hoping that once his brother's girlfriend delivered the baby, Thomas would completely open up.

"She's all I ever want," Daniel mumbled, then left his post to take long strides to Saige. Mr. Carter relinquished her into his possession.

"I'll take care of her, sir," Daniel reassured him and they exchanged a handshake.

"I know you will." He was physically overcome with emotion as he nodded and went to sit next to his wife.

Turning to Saige, Daniel took his time indulging in his bride's beauty. Then, with a sense of urgency, he hurried Saige to the altar and nodded for their minister to get started.

"Dearly beloved, we are gathered here today to join this man and woman in holy matrimony." Pastor Hogan asked, "Who gives this woman away?"

He and Saige glanced at her parents. Everyone patiently waited as her father helped Mrs. Carter to her feet.

"We in good faith happily give away our precious daughter into the loving care of Daniel," they said in unison, before retaking their seats.

Saige blew her a kiss and Daniel nodded, then they turned back to Pastor Hogan.

"The bride and groom have decided to write their vows," he informed their guests.

Taking Saige's hands in his, Daniel squeezed them. "Saige, you are my world. You possess a kindness and a sincerity within you that is infectious. As Jesus is my witness, I promise to love you, take care of you, respect you, and listen to you as my equal. I will cover you with my protection and I have forsaken all others for you—just you. I promise you my faithfulness." When a tear fell, Daniel caught it with his thumb. "I love you."

When it was Saige's turn, she began to tremble. Daniel gave her an encouraging smile. "I love you, Daniel. I never knew a stalker could turn out to be my best friend," she paused as others chuckled with them. "You're so incredible that you make it easy for me to love you and I promise to love you. I'll build you up when you feel weak, remind you of your strength, and obey you. More than anything, I promise you my faithfulness until death…" She swallowed, then whispered, "…do us part."

"It's all right, baby." Daniel wiped at her tears.

Continuing with the ceremony, Pastor Hogan admonished them of the seriousness of the vows they were making before God and their witnesses. "Brother Washington and Sister Carter, what God has joined together, let no man or woman come into your marriage and cause separation. By the power that God has vested in me and by the state of Missouri, I now pronounce you two individuals as one flesh to the glory of God." Closing his little book, the pastor faced Daniel. "Brother Washington, now declaring you husband and wife, you may now kiss Sister Washington."

As the cheers erupted around them, Daniel peeled back the veil that separated them. Saige's long lashes fluttered closed as his lips met hers. He sealed the deal with a tender kiss that sparked a longing that had lain dormant for months. Praise God the wait was over.

Reluctantly, Daniel stepped back, but couldn't resist wrapping Saige in his arms again and inhaling her faint perfume. "Love you. Forever and always."

She looked at him with such love shining in her eyes. "I need forever and always. I love you too."

Pastor Hogan reminded them of his presence with a booming declaration. "Ladies and gentleman, please welcome Mr. and Mrs. Daniel Washington."

Lifting their joined hands in the air, Daniel twirled his wife under his arm as if she were a princess—his.

Back from a short honeymoon at a bed & breakfast in the Lake of the Ozarks, Saige Washington could never have imagined this type of bliss, being married to Daniel. She liked being his wife. With the new status, Saige had gone overboard shopping for "his" and "hers" pillow cases, towels, bathrobes, and mugs, anything that had that imprint.

"So is this your new hobby, shopping for couple items," Maxi teased.

"Oh, no, Mr. Washington is my new hobby," Saige giggled as she met Maxi for lunch.

One of the many things she loved about Daniel was he took the lead in asking about her mother, visiting her, making sure they worked as a team, taking her mother to doctor's visits when she couldn't or running the simplest errands.

One night as they reclined on their condo's back patio, holding hands and watching the sunset, she faced him. "I know you love me unconditionally, but do you ever feel cheated inheriting my drama. I know that's not good to begin a marriage..."

"Shhh. Have I ever complained?"

Shaking her head, Saige answered, "No. I just want to make sure."

"Baby, I meant to ask you awhile back, but since you have so much free time in the summer from the university, have you ever thought about starting your own greeting card business online? You know I'll back you one-hundred percent. With my drafting skills, I could help create 3-D greeting cards with your inspirational phrases." He grinned eagerly.

Reaching over, Saige rubbed his smooth jaw. He had been a willing participant as she tried her hand at shaving him this morning. To her credit, she had only nicked him one time. She blushed when she recalled her punishment.

"I have thought about it, but American Greetings and Hallmark dominate the market, even their online e-cards don't generate a lot of revenue for them. At least I have visibility in the stores." She became quiet as her mother came to mind without warning. "I hope mom will be around this Christmas," she said softly.

"Me too. You've shown me the importance of family around the holidays." Daniel squeezed her hand, then brought it to his lips.

"But in the end, it's God's will in heaven that will be done on earth as we pray the 'Our Father' prayer."

"I'm glad that Mrs. Saige Washington is God's will for me." Daniel gently pulled her on his lap and kissed her.

Chapter 18

Christmas was in the air and Saige praised God every morning that her mother was still alive. But as the holiday drew closer, her mother refused any more chemo. The doctors agreed and recommended hospice.

Hospice—not them. Saige didn't know how long she cried after her father called her with the news. He also called Daniel. She was surprised that her husband had excused himself from an important meeting, left the office and drove to pick her up from her job.

When he walked into her office at the university, she ran into his arms and sobbed. The death angel was actually drawing near. "Let's go," he said and he drove straight to her parents' house. They would come back and get her car later.

Saige didn't get out the car right away when Daniel parked. She could only stare at her childhood home and wonder what it would be like without Adele Carter there. Per her mother's request, she demanded her father decorate the house for the holidays inside and out as usual.

"I left you with traditions, she had spoken softly the night she and Daniel were at the house cooking for

Thanksgiving when she had more strength. "Continue to follow them and you'll always have memories,"

Finally, Daniel coaxed her out of the car. Saige's legs were wobbly as he assisted her toward the front door. Walking into the living room, Saige saw an unfamiliar face sitting in a chair. She surmised the woman was with the hospice program.

Her father stood and hugged her. Saige released more tears, drenching his shirt. Daniel encircled them in a group hug. After a while, she composed herself and was able to meet the visitor, Nurse Redman.

With her husband on one side and her father on the other, Saige informed the hospice nurse, "All I want for Christmas is my mother." It was ten days away. Since her mother could no longer hold anything on her stomach, the countdown had begun. "Is that too much to ask? Is it?" Saige knew she was talking to the wrong person. The woman didn't have any power of life or death in her tongue.

Daniel rubbed her back as she rubbed her temples.

"God's grace has been sufficient for us," her father patted her shoulder.

The nurse shifted her body on the seat. "And God's grace may be extended to Christmas, Mrs. Washington. I know some may not believe it, but it's not uncommon for terminally ill patients to fight for each breath until a birthday, wedding, especially this time of year. I'm not necessarily religious, but I have seen some of God's grace."

"Thank you." Saige choked back tears then rested her head on Daniel's shoulder.

"Well Nurse Redman, we're a Bible-believing, praying family," her father stated. "And right at this moment, I feel the urge to pray and you are welcome to join in." When she consented, the four of them stood and joined hands, then bowed their heads.

"Lord, in the mighty name of Jesus, we come boldly before Your throne where we may obtain mercy and grace. I thank You for allowing me to have the love of my life for so many years. You have never forsaken us, You have always provided for us—food, shelter and even health. Even the doctors are amazed by her strength, but we know that her prolonged life with this condition has been because of Your grace. Jesus, You give and take away…" her father sniffed. "I give her back to You for Your safekeeping until I meet her again in the rapture. In the precious name of Jesus. Amen."

There wasn't a dry eye in the living room as they mumbled, "Amen."

After that day, Saige took family leave from her job. Daniel couldn't, but they stayed at her parents' house. And her mother-in-law came in town and stayed at their condo. Each day, Saige prayed that her mother would be there on Christmas.

On Christmas Eve, her mother was in and out of a sleepy state. Family and friends came by to softly sing hymns and pray. Maxi had the hardest time pulling Grace from her mother's side. She was inconsolable that she was losing her best childhood friend.

"It's all right," her mother's voice was faint. "Jesus gave me the victory. Oh, death where is thy sting?" she slurred 1 Corinthians 15:55.

When her mother grew too weak to open her eyes, she whispered a request that someone read her Scriptures about New Jerusalem. Like clockwork, the family honored her wishes. Her father went into the bedroom first, carrying the family Bible passed down from his grandfather to his father and then she and Daniel would have it eventually.

Saige watched from the doorway as her father scooted the chair closer to the bed and turned pages. In a soft storyteller voice, he began reading, "Revelation 20, verse one, '*Then I saw an angel coming down from heaven…*'"

Returning to the living room, Saige snuggled under Daniel on the sofa to keep a vigil. It was déjà vu that her parents had sat on the sofa like that many a day. "I'm really going to miss my mom, but I guess this really is like the Lion King's circle of life."

To be present in the body is to stand in My presence. Take comfort in My words, God's voice surrounded her in a cocoon until she drifted off to sleep.

Daniel didn't wake Saige when her father came out the room for the next reader. "In this life we are most miserable if we put our trust in man. God will take care of her. May you and my baby girl have a long life," her father said.

"Thank you, sir." Daniel nodded and carefully traded places with Mr. Carter who gave him the Bible to take the next reading shift.

The next morning, Mrs. Carter's eyes remained closed, but she mumbled, "Merry Christmas, my Savior is born and He's waiting for me."

"We know, Momma." Saige's eyes watered until the tears flowed. Thank You, Lord, for letting her be here."

The rest of Daniel's family had arrived in St. Louis and

came over to the Carters' house to pay their respects and keep them company during the vigil. The hospice nurse arrived and checked her mother's vitals. When Nurse Redman finished her service, she walked into the living room and immediately all conversation ceased.

"Any time now. Mrs. Carter could go tonight or tomorrow, but God did give her grace to be here with you this Christmas."

That night, Saige and her father climbed into the king size bed with her mother and Daniel slept in the recliner nearby. They waited for her mother to take her last breath.

Days later on New Year's Eve, Adele Carter made her transition with a smile on her face. The Homegoing service for Saige's mother was packed. The tiara Saige wore on her wedding day was placed on her mother's head. Truly, she was the bride for the Bridegroom to come. The Eulogy, songs, and remarks were lively as if they were in a revival. Jesus had literally dried the many tears from the family's eyes as they celebrated her mother's life.

Chapter 19

Life goes on. God made sure of that when months later, Saige learned that she was expecting. Finally, there were happy tears. Daniel went into pampering mode the moment they returned from the doctor's office.

Daniel watched his wife closely to gauge her moods. Saige still had bouts of crying, which was expected. It was hard on him, too, but he had to be strong for her. "How are you feeling about your mother missing the news of the baby?"

She stopped surfing the baby websites and gave him a glowing smile. "It's the Lion King's Circle of Life. I know how this story is going to go. With anticipation, I hope to become my mother."

Daniel winked. "And I pray that I will be a good daddy for my boy or little girl, or both." He wiggled his brows mischievously.

"Don't push it."

"I'm just sayin'." Daniel's father-in-law and his family were ecstatic to get the news about an addition to the family. Maxi and her mother began to dote on Saige as he was sure his mother-in-law would have done.

The weeks turned into months and Saige's pregnancy progressed without any complications and no twins to his wife's relief.

Things were also going smoothly at the firm. One afternoon, he and Jason were returning to the office from a job site and his friend asked, "Your wife's not around, so what are you having?"

The grin came first, then Daniel answered," A little girl. Saige doesn't know. She wants to be surprised, but I asked the OB doctor."

Slapping Daniel on the back, Jason grinned. "Man, you're so in trouble. Your wife is fine and her mother was a pretty lady. You know your daughter is going to be a knockout, right?"

"Of course!" Daniel pulled into the company's lot and parked. "So, it's countdown to August 30th."

Daniel didn't get a chance to baby his wife the last month of her pregnancy because his mother flew into St. Louis. Eloise Washington felt it was her God-given right job to dote on both of them.

One Sunday afternoon after the three of them had returned from church, Saige took a nap while he and his mother were in the kitchen, warming up dinner.

"You know, son, I'm glad we were able to get past our differences, or I may have missed this opportunity to spend time with my first daughter-in-law." She paused and rolled her eyes. "Because it's no telling when your brother will even get around to marrying Candi..." his mother went on a rampage about Thomas, finally seeing the light of what Daniel had been saying years earlier.

He stopped her. "Mom, I'm saved now. I hope I will be the example for Thomas to come to Christ. Not just him, but Phyllis and her family, and you. Even though it was heart-breaking to watch Mrs. Carter die when God took her away, He gave us a gift to fill her void— peace and a baby."

"I noticed that. Her funeral was one big celebration. I've never seen anything so joyous!"

Bowing his head, Daniel prayed, so he would say the right words. "So why didn't you go down the aisle for prayer as Pastor Hogan made the altar call today?" He had preached from 1 Thessalonians 4, the rapture chapter, as the saints called it.

"Honestly, I don't know. It seemed like that Scripture he read was relatable with Adele's passing."

"Promise me that the day you hear God's Voice, you'll answer—repent of spoken and unspoken sins and be baptized in water and in spirit in Jesus' name."

His mother didn't answer right away. "I will, son. You've been working on me for a while and I see the change God's made in your life. It would serve Thomas right if we go get saved and run the devil out of him."

On August 29th, Saige delivered a 6 pound 8 ounce little girl. Cuddling Dana Adele in her arms, she cooed at the baby with Daniel at her side. Their daughter could be mistaken for a doll, she was so beautiful.

"Two princesses. What more could a man ask for?" Daniel kissed Saige's cheek. "Thank you, baby."

It didn't take long for Dana to become the center of attention for the Washingtons and Carters. By the time

Dana turned three months old, she favored her grandmother, Adele.

Standing in the doorway of the nursery, Saige folded her arms and watched her father rock Dana who was already asleep. "Dad, what should we do about Christmas tradition this year?"

"You're married now. You and Daniel should create your own traditions and the in-laws can fit in somewhere." He glanced at his granddaughter and smiled.

Saige's heart ached for her father. At least her cousins, especially Derrick and Reggie had started to spend more time with him.

"Would you mind if Daniel and I spend Thanksgiving in Detroit and Christmas in St. Louis—at your house."

"I'd rather come here, if you and Daniel don't mind. I have something to look forward to here." He patted Dana on the back.

Chapter 20

The Wednesday before Thanksgiving, Daniel glanced out the window as their plane soared into the sky from St. Louis Lambert Airport. Dana was quietly sucking on her bottle in Saige's arms. Motherhood never looked so good on his wife.

And he figured if he was going to have any pride, it would be about the family God had given him. This would be his first Thanksgiving with his family in six years and the first time Dana would be visiting.

An hour and a half later, the plane touched down at Detroit's Wayne County Airport. Gathering his daughter in his arms, he walked off the plane with Saige close by his side. Daniel felt blessed. As they left the terminal en route to the baggage claim area, the balloons and signs caught his attention first before Dana noticed the group. This time, his brother was with them, holding his daughter, Tiffany, but there was no sign of Candi.

While everyone *ooh*ed and *ahh*ed over Dana, his daughter seemed more fascinated with the balloons.

"Look at Mommy and daughter. Don't you two look precious?" Phyllis complimented his wife's faux fur ball hat and fuchsia cashmere coat. Dana also had on the same color coat and matching hat.

"Thank you." Daniel answered for them.

"Not you. You always look the same." Phyllis rolled her eyes at him. "Makes me wish I had a little girl." She faked a pout as she reached for Dana who wouldn't go to her aunt.

Everyone laughed.

"Mommy, if you get a little girl, can we go live with Uncle Danny and Aunt Say?" Daniel's oldest nephew asked with a serious expression.

"Sure."

Lawrence jumped up and down and Ryan mimicked his older brother without a clue.

"Just kidding," Phyllis burst their bubble.

"Let's see if Dana will come to her Uncle Tommy." His brother reached for his daughter in an attempt to do an exchange. Surprisingly, Dana went without a fuss and so did Tiffany, who was a year older, go to Daniel. Thomas taunted the others, bragging about his charm as the group made their way to the baggage area.

Once at the house, his mother pulled Saige aside and gave her a longer hug than the one at the airport. "How you holding up, sweetie?"

"God is good." Saige nodded. All I know is I want to be a good mother, like my mother. I'm looking forward to celebrating my first Christmas as a mommy."

Daniel stepped away from the door, eavesdropping. Yes, everything would be all right. He lifted his hand in the air in praise and mouthed, *Thank You, Jesus.*

Before everyone retired to bed, his mother made an announcement. "I made some calls to area churches to see which ones have Thanksgiving service. I would like for us to start a new tradition and attend church to give God thanks." She gave Thomas a pointed look.

Thomas shrugged. "I guess it wouldn't hurt."

While some mumbled, "Amen," Daniel shouted, "Hallelujah."

Epilogue

A month later, Saige celebrated her first Christmas without her mother, but as a mother. Her spoiled brat made it hard pressed for her to be sad. Her house smelled of baked dishes, desserts, and turkey. Her father had helped, or rather supervised, Daniel with putting up the lights on the house and decorations inside.

Since her father spent the night with them, he was the first one up on Christmas morning.

Dana remained the center of attention as she grabbed for the wrapping paper, then tried to put it in her mouth. She seemed fascinated with Daniel's 3-D paper pop up doll he had designed especially for his daughter. Saige was wowed by the detail.

They were about to eat when her father handed her a gift she hadn't noticed. "What's this?" Saige asked as she admired the purple velvet covered square box. It was trimmed in gold pearls. "It's beautiful. She lifted the lid and gasped. She didn't have to finger the contents as her vision blurred. Turning to her father, her mouth shook as she tried to find her voice. "Momma kept these?"

"Yes," he said softly and gave her a hug. "Every single

greeting card you ever bought or made for her, Adele kept it. Before she got real sick, she gave me this box she had hid in the closet. She wanted me to give it to you the first Christmas she was gone and tell you that God had made room for your gift. Your Christmas Greetings has mended many hearts."

Daniel leaned over and brushed a kiss against her cheek. "And brought two hearts together. Merry Christmas, baby."

Book club discussion

1. Share your good holiday memories.
2. Which character were you drawn to?
3. What was the real meaning of Christmas? Reconciliation or the resurrection?
4. Have you ever found a greeting card that expresses exactly what you're feeling?
5. Did Saige ever get closure from her loss around the holidays?
6. Here is a challenge: Reach out to someone who shies away from holidays. It doesn't matter which one and show them love.

A special thank you for choosing *Christmas Greetings*. Merry Christmas and happy Resurrection Day!

I hope you loved it! Please take a few minutes to post a review on Amazon or Goodreads and sign up for my monthly newsletter at http://www.patsimmons.net. Thank you in advance.

Pat

About the Author

PAT SIMMONS is a self-proclaimed genealogy sleuth. She is passionate about researching her ancestors, then casting them in starring roles in her novels. She hopes her off-beat method will track down distant relatives who happen to pick up her books. She has been a genealogy enthusiast since her great-grandmother died at the young age of ninety-seven years old in 1988.

She describes the evidence of the gift of the Holy Ghost as an amazing, unforgettable, life-altering experience. She believes God is the author who advances the stories she writes.

Pat has a B.S. in mass communications from Emerson College in Boston, Massachusetts. She has worked in various media positions in radio, television, and print for more than twenty years. Currently, she oversees the media publicity for the annual RT Booklovers Conventions.

She is the author of nine single titles and several eBook novellas. Her awards include *Talk to Me,* ranked #14 of Top Books in 2008 that Changed Lives by *Black Pearls Magazine.* She is a two-time recipient of the Romance Slam

Jam Emma Rodgers Award for Best Inspirational Romance for *Still Guilty* (2010) and *Crowning Glory* (2011), and the first recipient of the Katherine D. Jones Award for grace and humility as an author. Her bestselling novels include *Guilty of Love* and the Jamieson Legacy series: *Guilty by Association*, *The Guilt Trip*, and *Free from Guilt*. *The Acquittal* was her 2013 release; *No Easy Catch* is her 2014 release.

Pat has converted her sofa-strapped, sports-fanatical husband into an amateur travel agent, untrained bodyguard, and GPS-guided chauffeur. They have a son and daughter.

Pat's interviews include numerous appearances on radio, television, blogtalk radio, blogs, and feature articles.

Visit www.patsimmons.net or email her at authorpatsimmons@gmail.com

Snail mail: Pat Simmons, P O Box 1077, Florissant, MO 63031

Other Christian titles include:

The Guilty series
Book I: *Guilty of Love*
Book II: *Not Guilty of Love*
Book III: *Still Guilty*

The Guilty Parties series
Book I: *The Acquittal*
Book II: *The Confession,*
Fall 2015

The Jamieson Legacy
Book I: *Guilty by Association*
Book II: *The Guilt Trip*
Book III: *Free from Guilt*

The Carmen Sisters
Book I: *No Easy Catch*
Book II: *In Defense of Love*

Making Love Work
Anthology
Book I: *Love at Work*
Book II: *Words of Love*
Book III: *A Mother's Love*

Love at the Crossroads
Book I: *Stopping Traffic*
Book II: *A Baby for*
Christmas
Book III: *The Keepsake*
Book IV: *What God Has*
for Me

Single titles
Crowning Glory
Talk to Me
Her Dress (novella)

Holiday titles
Love for the Holidays
(Three Christian novellas)
A Christian Christmas
A Christian Easter
A Christian Father's Day
A Woman After David's
Heart (Valentine's Day)
Christmas Greetings

LOVE AT THE CROSSROADS SERIES

STOPPING TRAFFIC, *Book I of Love at the Crossroads series.* Candace Clark has a phobia about crossing the street, and for good reason. As fate would have it, her daughter's principal assigns her to crossing guard duties as part of the school's Parent Participation program. With no choice in the matter, Candace be-grudgingly accepts her stop sign and safety vest, then reports to her designated crosswalk. Once Candace is determined to overcome her fears, God opens the door for a blessing, and Royce Kavanaugh enters into her life, a firefighter built to rescue any damsel in distress. When a spark of attraction ignites, Candace and Royce soon discover there's more than one way to stop traffic.

A BABY FOR CHRISTMAS, *Book II of the Love at the Crossroads series.* Yes, diamonds are a girl's best friend, but in Solae Wyatt-Palmer's case, she desires something more valuable. Captain Hershel Kavanaugh is a divorcee and the father of two adorable little boys. Solae has never been married and longs to be a mother. Although Hershel showers her with expensive gifts, his hesitation about proposing causes Solae to walk and never look back. As the holidays approach, Hershel must convince Solae that she has everything he could ever want for Christmas.

THE KEEPSAKE, *Book III Love at the Crossroads series.* Until death us do part...or until Desiree walks away. Desiree "Desi" Bishop is devastated when she finds evidence of her husband's affair. God knew she didn't get married only to one day have to stand before a judge and file for a divorce. But Desi wants out no matter how much her heart says to forgive Michael. That isn't easier said than done. She sees God's one acceptable reason for a divorce as the only opt-out clause in her marriage. Michael Bishop is a repenting man who loves his wife of three years. If only...he had paid attention to the red flags God sent to keep him from falling into the devil's snares. But Michael didn't and he had fallen. Although God had forgiven him instantly when he repented, Desi's forgiveness is moving as a snail's pace. In the end, after all the tears have been shed and forgiveness granted and received, the couple learns that some marriages are worth keeping

LOVE FOR THE HOLIDAYS SERIES

A CHRISTIAN CHRISTMAS, *Book I of Love for the Holidays anthology.* Christian's Christmas will never be the same for Joy Knight if Christian Andersen has his way. Not to be confused with a secret Santa, Christian and his family are busier than Santa's elves making sure the Lord's blessings are distributed to those less fortunate by Christmas day. Joy is playing the hand that life dealt her, rearing four children in a home that is on the brink of foreclosure. She's not looking for a handout, but when Christian rescues her in the checkout line; her niece thinks Christian is an angel. Joy thinks he's just another man who will eventually leave, disappointing her and the children. Although Christian is a servant of the Lord, he is a flesh and blood man and all he wants for Christmas is Joy Knight. Can time spent with Christian turn Joy's attention from her financial woes to the real meaning of Christmas—and true love?

A CHRISTIAN EASTER, Book II Love for the Holidays anthology, How to celebrate Easter becomes a balancing act for Christian and Joy Andersen and their four children.

Chocolate bunnies, colorful stuffed baskets and flashy fashion shows are their competition. Despite the enticements, Christian refuses to succumb without a fight. And it becomes a tug of war when his recently adopted ten year-old daughter, Bethani, wants to participate in her friend's Easter tradition.

Christian hopes he has instilled Proverbs 22:6, into the children's heart in the short time of being their dad.

A CHRISTIAN FATHER'S DAY, Book III Love for the Holidays anthology. Three fathers, one Father's Day and four children. Will the real dad, please stand up. It's never too late to be a father—or is it? Christian Andersen was looking forward to spending his first Father's day with his adopted children---all four of them. But Father's day becomes more complicated than Christian or Joy ever imagined. Christian finds himself faced with living up to his name when things don't go his way to enjoy an idyllic once a year celebration. But he depends on God to guide him through the journey.

MAKING LOVE WORK SERIES

Making Love Work, Book 1: A MOTHER'S LOVE. To Jillian Carter, it's bad when her own daughter beats her to the altar. She became a teenage mother when she confused love for lust one summer. Despite the sins of her past, Jesus forgave her and blessed her to be the best Christian example for Shana. Jillian is not looking forward to becoming an empty-nester at thirty-nine. The old adage, she's not losing a daughter, but gaining a son-in-law is not comforting as she braces for a lonely life ahead. What she doesn't expect is for two men to vie for her affections: Shana's biological father who breezes back into their lives as a redeemed man and practicing Christian. Not only is Alex still goof looking, but he's willing to right the wrong he's done in the past. Not if Dr. Dexter Harris has anything to say about it. The widower father of the groom has set his sights on Jillian and he's willing to pull out all the stops to woo her. Now the choice is hers. Who will be the next mother's love?

Making Love Work, Book 2 : LOVE AT WORK. How do two people go undercover to hide an office romance in a busy television newsroom? In plain sight, of course. Desiree King is an assignment editor at KDPX-TV in St. Louis, MO. She dispatches a team to wherever breaking news happens. Her focus is to stay ahead of the competition. Overall, she's easygoing, respectable, and compassionate. But when it comes to dating a fellow coworker, she refuses to cross that professional line. Award-winning investigative reporter Bryan Mitchell makes life challenging for Desiree with his thoughtful gestures, sweet notes, and support. He tries to convince Desiree that as Christians, they could show coworkers how to blend their personal and private lives without compromising their morals.

Making Love Work, Book 3: WORDS OF LOVE. Call it old fashion, but Simone French was smitten with a love letter. Not a text, email, or Facebook post, but a love letter sent through snail mail. The prose wasn't the corny roses-are-red-and-violets-are-blue stuff. The first letter contained short accolades for a job well done. Soon after, the missives were filled with passionate words from a man who confessed the hidden secrets of his soul. He revealed his unspoken weaknesses, listed his uncompromising desires, and unapologetically noted his subtle strengths. Yes, Rice Taylor was ready to surrender to love. *Whew.* Closing her eyes, Simone inhaled the faint lingering smell of roses on the beige plain stationery. She had a testimony. If anyone would listen, she would proclaim that love was truly blind.

TESTIMONY: *IF I SHOULD DIE BEFORE I WAKE.*
It is of the LORD's mercies that we are not consumed, because His compassions fail not. They are new every morning, great is Thy faithfulness. Lamentations 3:22-23, God's mercies are sure; His promises are fulfilled; but a dawn of a new morning is God' grace. If you need a testimony about God's grace, then If I Should Die Before I Wake will encourage your soul. Nothing happens in our lives by chance. If you need a miracle, God's got that too. Trust Him. Has it been a while since you've had a testimony? Increase your prayer life, build your faith and walk in victory because without a test, there is no testimony.

HER DRESS. (Stand alone) Sometimes a woman just wants to splurge on something new, especially when she's about to attend an event with movers and shakers. Find out what happens when Pepper Trudeau is all dressed up and goes to the ball, but another woman is modeling the same attire.

At first, Pepper is embarrassed, then the night gets interesting when she meets Drake Logan. *Her Dress* is a romantic novella about the all too common occurrence—two women shopping at the same place. Maybe having the same taste isn't all bad. Sometimes a good dress is all you need to meet the man of your dreams.

The Guilty Series

Kick Off

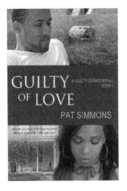

When do you know the most important decision of your life is the right one?

Reaping the seeds from what she's sown; Cheney Reynolds moves into a historic neighborhood in Ferguson, Missouri, and becomes a reclusive. Her first neighbor, the incomparable Mrs. Beatrice Tilley Beacon aka Grandma BB, is an opinionated childless widow. Grandma BB is a self-proclaimed expert on topics Cheney isn't seeking advice—everything from landscaping to hip-hop dancing to romance. Then there is Parke Kokumuo Jamison VI, a direct descendant of a royal African tribe. He learned his family ancestry, African history, and lineage preservation before he could count. Unwittingly, they are drawn to each other, but it takes Christ to weave their lives into a spiritual bliss while He exonerates their past indiscretions.

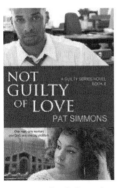

One man, one woman, one God and one big problem. Malcolm Jamieson wasn't the man who got away, but the man God instructed Hallison Dinkins to set free. Instead of their explosive love affair leading them to the wedding altar, God diverted Hallison to the prayer altar during her first visit back to church in years.

Malcolm was convinced that his woman had loss her mind to break off their engagement. Didn't Hallison know that Malcolm, a tenth generation descendant of a royal African tribe, couldn't be replaced? Once Malcolm concedes that their relationship can't be savaged, he issues Hallison his own edict, "If we're meant to be with each other, we'll find our way back. If not, that means that there's a love stronger than what we had." His words begin to haunt Hallison until she begins to regret their break up, and that's where their story begins. Someone has to retreat, and God never loses a battle.

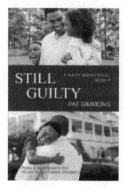

Cheney Reynolds Jamieson made a choice years ago that is now shaping her future and the future of the men she loves. A botched abortion left her unable to carry a baby to term, and her husband, Parke K. Jamison VI, is expected to produce heirs. With a wife who cannot give him a child, Parke vows to find and get custody of his illegitimate son by any means necessary. Meanwhile, Cheney's twin brother, Rainey, struggles with his anger over his ex-girlfriend's actions that haunt him, and their father, Dr. Roland Reynolds, fights to keep an old secret in the past.

Follow the paths of this family as they try to determine what God wants for them and how they can follow His guidance. Still Guilty by Pat Simmons is the third installment of the popular Guilty series. Read the other books in the series: Guilty of Love and Not Guilty of Love, and learn more about the Jamieson legacy in Guilty by Association, The Guilt Trip, and Free from Guilt. The Acquittal starts off the Guilty Parties series.

THE JAMIESON LEGACY SERIES

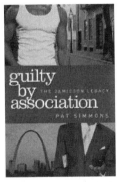

The Jamieson Legacy, Book I: *GUILTY BY ASSOCIATION*. How important is a name? To the St. Louis Jamiesons who are tenth generation descendants of a royal African tribe—everything. To the Boston Jamiesons whose father never married their mother—there is no loyalty or legacy. Kidd Jamieson suffers from the "angry" male syndrome because his father was an absent in the home, but insisted his two sons carry his last name. It takes an old woman who mingles genealogy truths and Bible verses together for Kidd to realize his worth as a strong black man. He learns it's not his association with the name that identifies him, but the man he becomes that defines him.

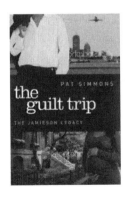

The Jamieson Legacy, Book II: *THE GUILT TRIP*. Aaron "Ace" Jamieson is living a carefree life. He's good-looking, respectable when he's in the mood, but his weakness is women. If a woman tries to ambush him with a pregnancy, he takes off in the other direction. It's a lesson learned from his absentee father that responsibility is optional. Talise Rogers has a bright future ahead of her. She's pretty and has no problem catching a man's eye, which is exactly what she does with Ace. Trapping Ace Jamieson is the furthest thing from Taleigh's mind when she learns she pregnant and Ace rejects her. "I want nothing from you Ace, not even your name." And Talise meant it.

 **The Jamieson Legacy, Book III:** *FREE FROM GUILT.* It's salvation round-up time and Cameron Jamieson's name is on God's hit list. Although his brothers and cousins embraced God—thanks to the women in their lives—the two-degreed MIT graduate isn't going to let any woman take him down that path without a fight. He's satisfied with his career, social calendar, and good genes. But God uses a beautiful messenger, Gabrielle Dupree, to show him that he's in a spiritual deficit. Cameron learns the hard way that man's wisdom is like foolishness to God. For every philosophical argument he throws her way, Gabrielle exposes him to scriptures that makes him question his worldly knowledge.

THE GUILTY PARTIES SERIES

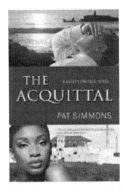

The Guilty Parties, Book I: *THE ACQUITTAL.* Two worlds apart, but their hearts dance to the same African drum beat. On a professional level, Dr. Rainey Reynolds is a competent, highly sought-after orthodontist. Inwardly, he needs to be set free from the chaos of revelations that make him question if happiness is obtainable. His father, the upstanding OB/GYN socialite is currently serving prison time after admitting his guilt in an old crime. His older sister refuses to move past the betrayal and attempts to use Rainey as a crutch, but her bitterness is only keeping the family at odds as his twin sister, Cheney Reynolds Jamieson, tries to rebuild a damaged relationship caused by decisions she made in the past. To get away from the drama, Rainey is willing to leave the country under the guise of a mission trip with Dentist Without Borders. Will changing his surroundings really change him? If one woman can heal his wounds, then he will believe that there is really peace after the storm.

Ghanaian beauty Josephine Abena Yaa Amoah returns to Africa after completing her studies as an exchange student in St. Louis, Missouri. She'll never forget the good friends she made while living there. She couldn't count Rainey in that circle because she rejected his advances for good causes. Josephine didn't believe in picking up the pieces as the rebound woman from an old relationship that Rainey seems to wear on his sleeve. Although her heart bleeds for his peace, she knows she must step back and pray for Rainey's surrender to Christ in order for God to acquit him of his self-inflicted mental torture. In the Motherland of Ghana, Africa, Rainey not only visits the places of his ancestors, will he embrace the liberty that Christ's Blood really does set every man free.

THE CARMEN SISTERS SERIES

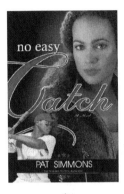

Book I: *No Easy Catch*. Shae Carmen hasn't lost her faith in God, only the men she's come across. Shae's recent heartbreak was discovering that her boyfriend was not only married, but on the verge of reconciling with his estranged wife. Humiliated, Shae begins to second guess herself as why she didn't see the signs that he was nothing more than a devil's decoy masquerading as a devout Christian man. St. Louis Outfielder Rahn Maxwell finds himself a victim of an attempted carjacking. The Lord guides him out of harms' way by opening the gunmen's eyes to Rahn's identity. The crook instead becomes infatuated fan and asks for Rahn's autograph, and as a good will gesture, directs Rahn out of the ambush!When the news media gets wind of what happened with the baseball player, Shae's television station lands an exclusive interview. Shae and Rahn's chance meeting sets in motion a relationship where Rahn not only surrenders to Christ, but pursues Shae with a purpose to prove that good men are still out there. After letting her guard down, Shae is faced with another scandal that rocks her world. This time the stakes are higher. Not only is her heart on the line, so is her professional credibility. She and Rahn are at odds as how to handle it and friction erupts between them. Will she strike out at love again? The Lord shows Rahn that nothing happens by chance, and everything is done for Him to get the glory.

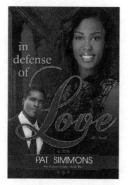

Book II: *In Defense of Love.* Lately, nothing in Garrett Nash's life has made sense. When two people close to the U.S. Marshal wrong him deeply, Garrett expects God to remove them from his life. Instead, the Lord relocates Garrett to another city to start over, as if he were the offender instead of the victim.

Criminal attorney Shari Carmen is comfortable in her own skin—most of the time. Being a "dark and lovely" African-American sister has its challenges, especially when it comes to relationships. Although she's a fireball in the courtroom, she knows how to fade into the background and keep the proverbial spotlight off her personal life. But literal spotlights are a different matter altogether.

While playing tenor saxophone at an anniversary party, she grabs the attention of Garrett Nash. And as God draws them closer together, He makes another request of Garrett, one to which it will prove far more difficult to say "Yes, Lord."